Nick F... Winni... ...g ... What He Wanted From More Formidable Opponents Than Someone Like Her.

She had no illusions about his invitation, but that didn't take away the temptation to accept.

"Stop worrying about my motives." He leaned forward and picked up her hand, placing his thumb on her wrist. "Your pulse is racing, as is mine." His strong fingers were warm, a steady, light pressure that made her heart beat faster. His brooding dark eyes bore a promise of sensuality.

"Say yes, Grace," he coaxed in a husky voice. "I'll take you home tonight, anytime you want. Let's have a few hours together."

"Yes," she whispered, "but I expect you to keep your promise of taking me home if I ask."

"I swear. I've never gone against a woman's wishes concerning a relationship."

"Don't. Don't describe dinner together as a 'relationship.' That would be a lie."

Dear Reader,

The powerful relationships between parent and child, grandparent and grandchild hold the potential to supercharge emotions. Two people in a volatile relationship complicate their lives, creating a dynamic situation where nerves are on edge. Love becomes a struggle between the compulsion to avoid someone and the desire to share passion.

Against the backdrop of the sophistication and wealth of a glittering Texas metropolis, this couple's emotions are ignited by the fiery passions they experience. A multimillionaire oil magnate, strong-willed Nick Rafford clashes with stunning Grace Wayland, who cares more for the baby entrusted to her care than for any amount of money. In this highly charged situation of opposing goals, Grace battles Nick while, at the same time, they combat an irresistible attraction.

This is a story of cold cash versus a warm heart, hot allure tempting cool logic. From the first moments of Nick's party, catered by Grace in his Dallas penthouse, the wild journey to love begins. Welcome to their story.

Sara Orwig

SARA ORWIG

TEXAS TYCOON'S CHRISTMAS FIANCÉE

Published by Silhouette Books

America's Publisher of Contemporary Romance

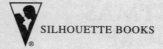 SILHOUETTE BOOKS

Recycling programs
for this product may
not exist in your area.

ISBN-13: 978-0-373-73062-9

TEXAS TYCOON'S CHRISTMAS FIANCÉE

SARA ORWIG

lives in Oklahoma. She has a patient husband who will take her on research trips anywhere from big cities to old forts. She is an avid collector of Western history books. With a master's degree in English, Sara has written historical romance, mainstream fiction and contemporary romance. Books are beloved treasures that take Sara to magical worlds, and she loves both reading and writing them.

Thank you to Krista Stroever. Also, with love to my family, who are my world. Love and thanks to Maureen.

One

Festive lights twinkled on Reunion Tower and across the sprawling metropolis of Dallas. Nick Rafford barely noticed his view. While he enjoyed guests at his party celebrating his return after being in Côte d'Azur the past three weeks, his attention focused on Grace Wayland, his caterer.

He had never seen her until tonight. His secretary had made arrangements for the catering company to do this Christmas party. From the first glimpse, Grace had surprised him.

Memory flashed back to the moment his butler had announced Grace's arrival and shown her into the penthouse study.

Rising to his feet, Nick suffered a jolt to his system as sea-green eyes met his gaze. For an instant she seemed equally startled because color drained from her face and her eyes widened. It was fleeting, vanishing when she regained her composure.

Grace Wayland's plain black dress should have caused her

to fade into anonymity. Instead, he was riveted as she crossed the room and held out a slender hand to shake his.

When his hand closed over hers, the contact sent a sizzling current. She stood only a few feet away and hot attraction engulfed him. Mere seconds or a minute—he didn't know how long their gazes remained locked. Breaking the spell, she said in a low voice, "I'm Grace Wayland."

Her name was enough to bring him out of his daze, causing his second surprise of the evening. Brilliant green eyes mirrored his own anger. He had anticipated a different response, expecting her to fawn over him, to do all she could to please him with this party. Curious about her cool manner, he studied her.

"And so I meet one of the Raffords," she added.

"You knew who I was before my secretary called about this party?"

"Of course," she said, removing her hand from his, warmth lingering from the slight physical contact. "I imagine you've heard about me, just as I certainly have you. We have something in common—Michael. That's who this is about, isn't it?"

Nick kept his features impassive, hiding his surprise at her bluntness. "I figured I'd be the one to bring up Michael. My party isn't the place or time for a discussion. Will you be available if I come to your office Monday?"

"Fine. I'll be free around nine. How's that time?"

"I can be there at nine," he said, having already cleared his Monday calendar in anticipation of meeting with her.

"I assumed Michael was why you paid an exorbitant fee to get me to cater tonight. You could have saved yourself money by coming to me directly to book the party," she added, her voice dropping to a whisper.

He shrugged. "You were highly recommended and I thought this was a way to meet. Tonight, my focus is on my party," he said, suspecting it was going to be difficult to keep his mind on his party or his guests with Grace around. As he'd answered her, he noticed her full, rosy, inviting lips.

"When it comes to Michael, to my baby, I doubt we have anything to discuss," she declared.

His surprise over her responses deepened. Mixed reactions were churning inside. He wanted to remind her that her "my baby" remark had been inaccurate, but he restrained himself from antagonizing her unnecessarily. His annoyance battled his attraction. Once more, their gazes collided, the heated moment stretching until she broke the spell.

"I have your instructions regarding the party. My help is waiting in the van to bring in the food and get ready."

"I detect reluctance about catering for me," he said.

"This job will be good for my business," she replied, the barrier of coolness still in place.

"Summon your help. I'll have someone show you around," he said, while he considered her professional, noncommittal answer. Nick walked to the intercom to talk briefly to his butler, who responded in seconds. As Grace left with him, Nick watched her walk out, noticing her long legs and narrow waist.

Casually, while guests arrived and mingled, he checked on the arrangements, finding food, setups—every aspect of the preparations—flawless and accomplished with no disruption to him.

Later in the evening he stood with his two closest friends. He was only half-listening to their conversation while he watched Grace replenish a dish on his dining table.

"I don't blame you for paying little attention to us," Tony Ryder, Nick's tall, curly-haired friend, said. "Where did you find her? The hors d'oeuvres are excellent, but I don't think it would matter how the food tasted if she came along with it. Is she the manager?"

"Manager and owner. It's a small business I heard about, so I thought I'd try it."

"Right," remarked Jake Benton, his blue-eyed gaze flicking to Grace and back to Nick. "How soon are you taking her out?"

Nick shook his head. "I don't think so. So how has the basketball game been while I've been away?"

"Team missed you," Jake said. "Hope you're not too out of shape after a month off."

"Given the amateurs we are and playing twice a month at best, I don't think my missing a couple of games will matter except for the score of our team," Nick remarked, and his friends laughed.

"Great party, Nick," a tall, blue-eyed man said as he joined the three. "Missed you at the last game."

"See, Gabe agrees. The team needs you," Jake said.

Nick faced Jake's younger brother. "I don't think I'm all that important. I'm not giving up my trips for basketball with the three of you," he added, and the others grinned.

As they talked about their hobby, Nick tried to keep his attention on his friends. They had known him long enough that they would notice if he continued to watch Grace. Both Tony and Jake were as close to him as brothers. Gabe was close also, since he had grown up with them. Nick knew he could trust all three if he told them about Grace, but he didn't care to discuss Michael with anyone.

He didn't want to discuss his nephew with Grace either, but he had to. Later during the party, when she was in the kitchen, he strolled in to find her refilling a tray of hors d'oeuvres.

After a glance at him she returned her attention to the job at hand. "I hope everything is satisfactory."

"More than acceptable," he replied, watching her long fingers move, deftly arranging bruschetta, mini quiches, enticing tidbits on the tray. Even though her hands bore no rings, he already knew her single status. He caught a whiff of an unfamiliar, exotic perfume. Too much about her enticed him to the point he forgot his mission for minutes at a time. When had he found a woman as distracting as Grace?

"You're very good at this, yet you've only been doing it a few years," he said, taking a tasty cheese phyllo she had just placed on a silver tray. Replacing it immediately, she continued working.

"As I expected, you've inquired about my background," she remarked without looking up. The light glinted on gold highlights in her silky brown hair worn clipped in a loose bun on her head. "I've worked in restaurants or in catering since I was in high school." Her long brown lashes hid her eyes as she worked.

"So this catering business of yours, is it a childhood wish come true?"

"Not exactly, but close," she answered. Big green eyes jolted him as they had at his first encounter. The crystal, vivid green beneath the long lashes was a stunning combination. Each look burned with a simmering animosity. He had to concede to himself that her beauty complicated his mission in spite of having nothing to do with the problem between them.

"You've done an excellent job tonight. You've impressed my friends."

"Thank you," she answered.

He left, fighting the urge to flirt with her, because that would be the road to disaster. He remained astounded by her aloof manner. He had never anticipated it. Her coolness made him reassess his view of her. Her poise and self-assurance denied her impoverished background. While she demonstrated little gratitude for his business, the catering had been executed with perfection. She loomed a more formidable foe than he had imagined.

"I don't have any idea what the deal is, Nick," Jake said,

walking up to him. "Anyone can feel the sparks when you and your caterer are together, yet the looks she gives you contradict that."

"You've forgotten," Nick said. "I told you about my brother and this baby he supposedly fathered."

"I remember," Jake said, turning to look again at Grace. "So this woman is the guardian?"

"Yes. I keep expecting Dad to revert to his old self and forget this nonsense about wanting a grandchild in the family, but so far he hasn't. He wants the baby to have our name and be in his life. He doesn't expect or want to have complete custody."

"He's older, Nick, and he's had a brush with mortality. That can change a man."

"This is totally out of character for him. Dad's thinking isn't as clear as it was before the last heart attack."

Jake sipped his drink and frowned slightly. "On other subjects or just this one?"

"I'll admit, mostly this one, but I'll repeat, this interest in a baby is so unlike him."

As a mutual friend approached, Nick turned to greet him and the conversation switched to golf, yet Nick couldn't lose his continual awareness of Grace. Occasionally, he looked into her green eyes and each time, electricity zigzagged through him. Certain he had the pertinent facts about her, he had been surprised there was no man in her life.

Thinking she would be impressed by the family wealth, he was still surprised by her frosty manner. His stubborn father would not back down. If she was uncooperative, they would be in for a battle, and he was the one in the middle who would have to do the negotiating. Normally, where a beautiful, single woman was involved, he would be happy to step in, but in the current situation, he opposed what his father wanted. Maybe Grace herself would settle the whole thing and for once in his life, the old man would have to accept not getting what he wanted.

Nick's spirits lifted only slightly. He hated to break the news to his father, who was frail now and in failing health. Eli had spent a lifetime getting his way and didn't take it well when he couldn't. Monday morning, Nick would discover where they stood.

A piano player filled the evening with music and conversation grew louder after everyone had eaten their fill.

In spite of enjoying his guests, Nick kept track of Grace, who remained in the background assisting and directing the cleanup. He had been watching her talk to one of her staff but then a guest took his attention and the next time he looked for Grace, she was nowhere in sight. The catering staff had disappeared as well. He excused himself and strolled through the crowd, entering an empty kitchen.

He saw an envelope with his name neatly typed on the front. The bill was inside and she had gone. He tapped the envelope against his palm. She hadn't been the woman he had expected. What would an appointment with her Monday bring?

Shivering from the cold winter night, Grace drove away from the high-rise condo where Nick resided in an exclusive, gated area near downtown Dallas. She heaved a sigh of relief. Visions of dark chocolate-colored, thickly lashed eyes bedeviled her. Nick Rafford was charismatic, overwhelming, sexy, and accustomed to getting what he wanted. Each time she had been near him tonight there had been a disturbing electricity between them. What woman wouldn't feel tempted around a man that attractive?

She had tried to hide her initial shock when she had entered the room to meet him. It was the first time she had seen one of the Rafford men in person. She had seen pictures and knew

Michael had their black hair and dark eyes, but in person, she noticed more. Michael and his uncle had the same straight nose and thick eyelashes, a dimple in the right cheek. The seven-month-old baby under her guardianship bore a strong resemblance to his uncle. Michael had good genes.

As she drove, she recalled glimpses of Nick smiling, laughing with friends, shaking hands, talking earnestly. He was breathtaking, handsome, too appealing. His white shirt with flashing gold cuff links and navy slacks added to his commanding appearance and there had been no mistaking his arrogance. The man made it obvious that he expected to have his wishes granted.

What did Nick really want? Was he coming after Michael? Another chill ran down her spine. Yet the coldness vanished as she continued thinking about Nick. No one could stay chilled remembering Nick.

She didn't want the Raffords in Michael's life. She admitted to herself she was terrified they would take the precious boy from her. She'd had him from the moment he left the hospital after his birth and loved him as if he were her own son. She mulled over the strong resemblance to his uncle. His incredibly handsome uncle.

Her fears had heightened when she had stepped into Nick's ritzy condo with its glass walls in the living area and panoramic views of the city. The opulent furniture and lamps were expensive. The kitchen had been state-of-the-art and when she had stepped into a spacious bathroom, the mirrors, plants and sunken tub with gold fittings had been as luxurious as the rest of the condo. She remembered seeing a spread about his home in a Dallas magazine. Imported marble, a New York decorator, priceless antiques, original oils, a lavish backdrop that added to his aura of wealth and power.

She wished she could shake Nick out of her thoughts, hoped even more that she would never see him again.

When she entered her small ground-floor apartment, she greeted her aunt, who was babysitting Michael.

Dressed in a gown and robe, Clara Wayland brushed brown hair away from her sleepy green eyes. "How was it?"

"The job went well. He seemed pleased."

"And?"

"And I have an appointment with him at my office Monday morning. Otherwise, I'm as uninformed as ever about what he wants. Well, maybe I know a little more, since I've actually met him. I'll tell you about it after I change clothes and look in on Michael. How was he tonight?"

"An angel. A happy baby who went to sleep about nine."

"I've missed him."

"You always do," her aunt said as Grace went into her bedroom, shedding clothes and changing into cotton pajamas and a robe. She tiptoed over to look at the crib, fighting the urge to pick up the sleeping baby and hold him in her arms. A chill gripped her. There could be no good reason Nick Rafford wanted to meet her. None. She didn't want him near Michael. She gazed at the baby, so aware of the startling resemblance to Nick. She leaned down to brush Michael's cheek with a light kiss and caught a whiff of baby powder. "You're mine now, sweetie. Not the Raffords'," she whispered.

She rejoined Clara, who had fixed cups of hot chocolate. "Monday morning, you can call your lawyer to go with you," Clara said.

"I won't need a lawyer to just talk to the man. Tonight is the first we've met."

Clara sighed. "I need to remember that you won't let him intimidate you or frighten you into doing something you don't have to do."

"I don't think that will happen," Grace said. "He was courteous. Obviously, he wants something concerning Michael. He hired my catering service to scope me out."

"Don't borrow trouble," Clara said.

"When Bart Rafford kicked Alicia out, he didn't want anything to do with his baby. He denied the baby was his. I can't imagine the jet-setting multimillionaire uncle has any interest in Michael. His brother never did and since Bart wasn't killed until Michael was three months old, he had time to meet his son if he'd wanted."

"Does the uncle have a wife and children?" Clara asked.

"No. Nick is single," Grace said, remembering his dark brown eyes on her as he grasped her hand in their handshake. "He's in society pages, so that's how I know he isn't married. He's busy and has a reputation as shrewd in business. From what Alicia told me, at that time, the grandfather had no interest in Michael and I've heard the grandfather's health has failed lately. An ailing grandfather, a single uncle—those are the only relatives. I can't figure out what, but they want something from me concerning Michael. I'll learn what it is on Monday morning."

"Please call me the first chance you get. I'll be worried about you."

"Don't fret," Grace said, smiling at Clara. "Legally, Michael is mine."

"Grace, the Raffords have an enormous fortune. You wouldn't stand a chance of stopping them if they—"

"Don't think about it," Grace said.

"You're right." Clara smiled. "I think I'll turn in. I wish you'd sleep in your room and let me take the sofa here."

"I'm fine. Thanks for staying tonight."

"I love to see Michael. You're the daughter I never had. My boys are scattered and still single—Chet in Germany. Miles in Japan. I've given up on my own grandkids, but thank goodness I can be with Michael."

"Chet sent you plane tickets and you'll be in Germany with him for Christmas."

"That's not like having them here," Clara said. "I worry about leaving you and Michael alone for Christmas."

"Don't be silly. You'll have a wonderful time and Glenda is already lined up to babysit Michael for me. I don't worry when he's with either one of you."

"She's reliable and she loves him, too. Glenda and I have been friends since we were five years old. She's like a sister to me," Clara said, repeating what Grace had heard many times before.

"Her family is coming Christmas day, so that's worked out," Clara added. She smiled at Grace. "Thank heavens I have you and Michael. I count my blessings every day." Clara hugged Grace and headed for her room. At the door she paused. "Bart Rafford killed in a ski accident. You wonder what would have happened had he lived."

"I suspect it would have been just the same as it is now."

"He never saw his son." Shaking her head, Clara left.

In minutes Grace was stretched beneath covers on the sofa. She lay in the dark, thinking about Nick's party, going back to the first moments, now etched in her memory. She couldn't forget Nick or anything about him. Nor could she keep from worrying about his purpose in seeing her. She wasn't giving up Michael no matter what, but the Rafford money and Nick's reputation as a ruthless, shrewd businessman worried her.

At nine Monday morning Nick was ushered into Grace's narrow, plain office. Looking dynamic, he dominated the space. Was it his take-charge attitude or his mere physical presence that sped up her heart rate? When she looked into his eyes, a current zinged to her toes. He was sinfully handsome and it was easy to see why women were drawn to him. She had watched him Friday night, occasionally hearing conversations as she passed him, and knew he could turn on the charm. With an effort she tore her gaze from his dark eyes.

As he glanced around, she became acutely conscious of her office with its cramped space and old furniture in the aging building. She operated on a shoestring, yet her business was growing, a plus, she reminded herself constantly.

"Good morning," she said, greeting Nick without offering her hand.

"Good morning," he replied, giving her a faint smile. "Red becomes you."

"Thank you," she replied. She was certain the compliment rolled off his tongue without thought, yet she couldn't keep from being pleased. He extended the envelope that had contained her bill and she guessed it was her payment.

"Here's for the party. You did a bang-up job and there were a lot of compliments on the food. You should get more bookings from my friends." His hand was well shaped, his fingers long, his white shirt cuffs hiding his wrists.

"Thank you. Some guests asked for my card. I appreciate the opportunity of your business," she replied. Approval would have been satisfying from any other customer, but his solemn expression and the intensity of his dark eyes took away pleasure. His presence screamed a mission. "Please have a seat."

He sat in one of the small chairs and she pulled one around to face him, too aware of his proximity. Unsettling, he threatened her well-being. Adding to his overpowering presence, his thickly lashed dark brown eyes were piercing.

"I've come to talk about Michael."

She drew a quick breath. "From the first I figured that was why you wanted to meet."

"That's right. My father is in poor health. In the past year he's had two heart attacks. Illness has changed his outlook on life. He'd like to meet you and Michael."

Her heart lurched and she locked her fingers together as she fought a sense of panic. The Raffords' power loomed. She imagined that the father was even more formidable than the son because of his years developing influential friends. Taking a quick breath, she attempted to maintain a calm demeanor.

"Are you aware that your brother signed away his rights to Michael?"

"That's what I've been told."

"He did that in the last weeks of Alicia's life. She tried to get everything lined up so Michael would be financially provided for and have a guardian until he's grown. I can't imagine your father simply wants to see the baby. I'd guess there's more to it than that," she added, hoping for a denial. When Nick didn't give one immediately, her dread increased.

"He doesn't intend to take Michael from you, but he wants to get acquainted with his grandson," Nick said. "I'll repeat—illness has changed my father's values. His grandson has become important to him. I'd like to arrange a meeting and it would be easier on my dad if you could get together at his house," Nick continued. Her gaze dropped to his mouth and slightly sensual lower lip. What would it be like to feel those lips against hers?

Startled by her train of thoughts, she returned to the moment. She could not keep from having a faint glimmer of hope from Nick's remarks. "If your father is that frail, he surely can't want Michael in his life much of the time. It doesn't sound as if he is in any shape to care for a baby."

"He's not, but he can afford to hire care. Frankly, while you have a growing, successful business," Nick said, glancing around her office, which she could imagine he was contrasting with his own and his father's, "my father can do much more financially for Michael than you can."

"Money really isn't everything," she replied. Her chill intensified. Nick sat relaxed, looking as if he was the one in charge. His tone of voice carried a note of steel, indicating she could be in for a bitter, ugly fight with a powerful man.

"I love Michael and when I'm not with him, my aunt, or her closest friend, keeps him. My flexible schedule allows me to spend a lot of hours with Michael. Did your parents spend hours with you?"

"Touché," Nick said with a trace of amusement. "No, they did not."

"I've read about you and your father in the society pages of the paper and local magazines. Your father has had several marriages and many women in his life. It was the same for your brother when he was alive. Who did you spend the most time with—nannies?"

"Nannies, the chauffeur, boarding school," Nick replied, confirming her guess. She wondered about his life and could see how his relationships might be shallow and brief. Some people would envy Nick's childhood, but she thought it was inadequate. She didn't want Michael to grow up in any such manner.

"Face the facts, you're limited in the life you can provide for Michael," Nick stated. "You should give some thought to what you're turning down here. My dad wants me to set up a meeting where he can talk to you about Michael. Just talk. You should be willing to do that, because there is nothing threatening in meeting. Far from it," Nick added, self-assurance lacing his tone. He remained at ease, as if assured of the outcome of this conversation.

She bristled. "Your brother wanted nothing to do with his baby. Where was your father at that time?"

"I've told you, my father is a changed man."

"This transformation is a little late and it's difficult for me to believe he's actually changed. Michael's mother, Alicia Vaughan, was my best friend my entire life. Before she died, she told me about Bart. When she was pregnant, your brother was blunt and coldhearted with Alicia. The last time Alicia saw him, he called her foul names while insisting he wanted nothing to do with 'her brat.' He sent her on her way in tears in a rainstorm. That night was when she had the wreck that eventually ended her life. She almost lost Michael because of the wreck. After what occurred, I can't see any reason to take Michael to your father."

Nick leaned forward, placing his arms on his knees, his navy suit jacket falling open. A gold cuff link glinted in the light. He was close, distracting her with fleeting thoughts about how handsome he was. She found it difficult to get her breath, impossible to resist looking again at his mouth. What was the man like when he was not on a mission? She had seen glimpses of that last night.

"My father has aged a lot in the past year. He's in failing health—I think he's hanging on for Christmas and he wants to see his grandson. Can't you at least meet with him? What harm could there be in that? You need to think about this, because you might be a lot better off and the baby certainly would. My father is enormously wealthy. Don't cut Michael off from a better life."

The words were persuasive, as well as the man. She felt a flutter of sympathy that vanished when she remembered Alicia sobbing in the hospital bed, hooked to tubes, hanging on to life. At the same time Michael, who was delivered a month early because of the car wreck, had been in neonatal intensive care. All caused in part because of how cold and harsh Bart Rafford had been to her friend.

"Michael was orphaned because of your brother. Alicia begged him to recognize his son. He could have said no without being hurtful about it. I see no point in taking Michael to visit your father. He's had his chance to have the baby in his life. He could have come forward when Alicia was pregnant or right after that last time she saw Bart."

Grace stood and Nick came to his feet immediately. She was aware of his height and that aura about him conveying his control. He stood close to her, and once again she was more conscious of Nick than anything else. His features were impassive and she had no idea whether he was irritated, disappointed or mapping his next move.

"Just because my brother was hurtful doesn't mean you should be. If you're frightened about Michael, don't be. My father can't take him from you, because he's not well enough to do so."

"I think I've made my feelings clear," she said, unable to get Alicia out of her mind or stop worrying that while Eli Rafford wasn't well, he was a man who had enough power to achieve his goals.

"You can live with your conscience over your decision?"

"Better than I could if I agreed to take Alicia's baby to see your father. Does he have any idea how cruel his son was to my friend? Or does he just want Michael in his life and he doesn't care what happened to Alicia? Bart used her and then discarded her."

"I think most women my brother 'used' were extremely willing as well as pleased at the time," Nick remarked drily, stirring Grace's indignation "Your friend wasn't forced to have an affair with him."

"She realized what a mistake she had made." Grace stepped away from Nick to head toward the door. "I think we've finished our conversation."

"Don't be so quick to toss away Michael's future. Suppose this catering business doesn't last? Then what?" Nick asked, honing in on her deep fear. "You know how to reach me if you change your mind," he said. As far as she could tell, he didn't seem distressed, but she suspected he could easily hide his feelings.

"I can tell you now—I won't change my mind."

Nick gave her a cool, satisfied smile as if he expected her

to capitulate to his wishes. "When you do rethink Michael's future, just call." Nick hesitated, his gaze undergoing a subtle change that warmed her. He gave her a glance that caused her heart to skip a beat.

"Too bad we didn't meet under other circumstances," he said in a deeper tone, this time setting her heart racing. As he left, closing the door, she let out her breath.

"But we didn't," she said to no one, surprised by his last remark which, for a brief moment, had taken her away from the problem. How much more difficult it was to deal with the situation when the messenger was a charismatic, sexy man like Nick.

She felt completely wrung-out, as if she had been sparring with a formidable foe. She didn't imagine she had seen the last of the Raffords. Men with wealth such as theirs did not accept defeat easily.

Was she cutting Michael off from a myriad of marvelous opportunities that Eli Rafford could provide? That was exactly what had sent Alicia to see Bart. Would Alicia have jumped at this chance and think Grace was being a poor guardian? Grace simply feared the Rafford patriarch would take Michael from her, but she needed to give Nick's request more consideration before she totally slammed the door on the Raffords. Eli Rafford could insure Michael's future. After a few days, it still wouldn't be too late to contact Nick and agree to his wishes.

The thought chilled her more.

She wanted no part of Eli Rafford and she couldn't imagine that he merely intended to see Michael a few times. She suspected he wanted his small grandson. And he would want to give him the life he had given Nick—nannies, chauffeurs and boarding schools. As far as she was concerned, she could give Michael vastly more because he would have her loving care and attention.

She walked around her desk and looked up her attorney's phone number, afraid she would need help to fight this battle. Frightened and concerned, she was certain it wasn't over and that she had not seen the last of Nick.

<u>Two</u>

Nick drove his black sports car away from the strip mall where Grace rented space for her office. Relief dominated his feelings as he glanced at his watch. His lunch appointment with his closest friends would get his mind off this problem for the time being.

Jake and Tony were already waiting and soon Gabe Benton joined them. Over hamburgers, Nick realized the lunch was not pushing his problem out of mind.

"Nick, I don't think you heard a word I said," Jake stated.

"Sorry," Nick answered. "It's Dad and what he wants. Long story, but the three of you know about the baby that might be Bart's. Dad has a bee in his bonnet about getting the baby into the Rafford family."

"And that's not what the baby's guardian wants," Tony guessed.

"Money talks. I can't imagine your dad hasn't made her an

offer or had you make her an offer," Jake remarked. "That's the usual MO for all our dads."

"She's not interested."

"Is this the new caterer you had?" Tony asked.

"As a matter of fact, yes."

"Simple. Just marry her," Jake suggested with a twinkle in his eyes.

Nick gave him a look. "I'm not marrying anyone to get something for Dad. I'm not marrying for years, period. All you guys will be married before I am."

"The hell you say," Tony replied. "Name your price, I'll bet you're married first."

Nick relaxed, enjoying the good-natured exchange and getting his mind off his problem. "I will be the last. One million in the pot."

"Oh, no. I'm definitely going to be the holdout. I'll bet a million and I will win," Jake said.

"I'm guaranteed to win," Tony stated.

"You guys—betting a million over getting married. I could be the winner because I'm the youngest, but my money is going elsewhere," Gabe said. "Count me out of this."

"All right," Nick said. "We have a bet. Last one to marry gets one million from the other two—namely, I will collect from both of you."

"Deal," Jake said as Tony nodded. "It's sweet," Jake added. "Gabe is our witness. I don't expect this bet to be over for years."

"You guys are in it now, and it will be years," Nick said, smiling and relaxing.

Their conversation shifted to sports and for half an hour he didn't think about Grace, the baby or his father. It wasn't until he told his friends goodbye and left that he went back to thinking about his father's demands.

"Might as well get this over now," he said to himself,

dreading breaking the news to his father. He changed direction and headed to his father's palatial estate. When he entered the grounds, he called his dad's nurse to let her know he was coming.

Circling splashing fountains, assorted statues and well-tended beds of flowers, Nick drove around the mansion to the back, sitting in the car long enough to call his office and tell them when he would be in.

He pushed the bell at the back and the door was opened by a gray-haired uniformed woman he had known since childhood.

"Good morning, Miss Lou," Nick said, smiling at her.

"Morning to you, Mr. Nick. Your father will be glad to see you."

"I have doubts about that. I'm telling him something he doesn't want to hear."

She laughed. "None of your escapades now!"

"There hasn't been any such nonsense since I went off to college," he said, laughing with her.

She chuckled and shook her head. "He's in the library. He'll be glad to see you. I think he's lonesome. He talks to me a lot more now."

"Then he shouldn't be so lonesome. You're good company," Nick said, smiling at her. He walked down the broad terrazzo-floored hall to enter the spacious room that included three walls of shelves filled with books and pictures.

His father was in a chair near the bay windows and his nurse turned to smile at Nick as she stood.

"Good morning."

"Hi, Megan. Morning, Dad," Nick said, crossing the room. "Megan, you can stay. I won't be here long," he said, but she shook her head.

"I have some things I can do," she said.

Nick watched the petite auburn-haired nurse as she left

through the open door into the hall. Nick sat facing his father, who was dressed and had shaved, wearing a cardigan over his shirt and with his feet in slippers. He was a thinner version of his old self and more gray had spread through his thick black hair. Nick knew he resembled his father and wondered if this was how he would look someday.

"How are you this morning?" Nick asked.

"Same as last week. I take it you've talked to Grace Wayland."

"Yes, I did. I went to her office today to discuss Michael."

"So when do I get to see my grandson?"

"Dad, because of Alicia, Grace has very strong feelings about us. She resents Bart's treatment of Alicia, especially Alicia's last visit with Bart."

A pained look crossed his father's face and his gaze shifted to the windows. Nick noticed a muscle working in his dad's jaw while he crushed the corner of his open cardigan in one hand. "I'm sorry I didn't talk to Bart more at the time. I made a mistake in not taking an interest from the first."

"Grace is bitter over her friend. She sees no point in bringing Michael to see you."

"Damn it, Nick! You can be persuasive. Why didn't you talk her into a meeting?"

"Well, maybe my heart wasn't in it. Stop and think a minute about it. We're not certain this is Bart's child."

"He told me that it probably was his baby. Early on, I didn't feel strongly about it, but my life has changed. I want to see my grandson. This is vital to me," his father snapped, some of the old force returning to his voice. He stood and walked to the mantel to brace his arm on it. "I want that child in the family. I intend to see that he has the family name." Eli turned to stare at Nick. "Doesn't she realize it will be better for Michael?"

"I pointed out to her that you can do a lot more for Michael than she will ever be able to," Nick said patiently, knowing there would be more to come because his father never gave up on something he wanted badly.

"She's not thinking about the baby."

"That doesn't matter if she refuses to allow you to see him. Bart signed away his rights. He gave up any claim. Add to that, Grace's bitter feelings over the treatment her friend received from Bart."

"I suppose she blames Bart for Alicia's wreck."

"She probably does," Nick said, mindful that Grace did blame Bart. "Dad, give it up. Someday I'll give you grandchildren. Besides, you've told me that you never wanted more children, nor did any of the women you married. It's a late point in life to decide you want to enjoy a grandchild."

"Nick, damn it, I intend to give my grandson his heritage of the Rafford name and in some manner to rectify what Bart did."

"You'll send your blood pressure higher worrying over this," Nick said gently. "Right now, you're not completely well. You can't deal with a grandbaby. You really never have wanted to have babies around."

"No, I haven't. I just want to see the little boy. I want him legally an heir—and I've told you that you will get the bulk of the estate no matter what happens. I wouldn't think of cutting you out of most of what I possess, but there is enough for him to have a trust. After all, Nick, he is your nephew."

"It's difficult to relate to a baby I've never seen, with a deceased mother I can't recall meeting." Stretching out his long legs, Nick folded his hands, giving his father time to vent his frustration.

"Bart handled things badly, but I'm aware of this family's responsibility—"

"Dad, you don't have a responsibility. Bart signed his away totally."

Eli scowled, glaring at his son. "I want this baby in our family and I can do so much for him."

"Grace Wayland doesn't want you to. She doesn't want you to meet him. She refused to see you. I'm sorry, but there it is."

"The hell you say? You walked out and gave up? You don't give up when it's something you want."

"Understand, Grace was adamant about it. She's incensed over her friend. She isn't going to be talked into it."

"Well, then I'll bribe her into it. Did you tell her I would set up a trust for Michael?"

"I told her you could do many beneficial things for him. I pointed out to her that you can do far more for Michael than she can and it didn't move her. She doesn't want nannies or chauffeurs or boarding schools for him."

"Damn it, what's the matter with the woman? She's in business for herself. You told me she came from a poor background with no college education in the family. How can she turn up her nose at money for the baby?"

"She's unhappy with the Raffords," Nick reaffirmed patiently.

"Alicia came from that same poor background, but she appreciated money."

"I can imagine," Nick remarked drily, thinking his brother got tangled up often with women after his money. "In a way, it's refreshing to meet a woman who doesn't put the dollar first."

"Refreshing? It's damned stubborn. She's letting emotions cloud her judgment and she isn't giving the baby a fair shake."

"She was unmovable," Nick said, hanging on to patience. "Maybe if I try again in a few months she will have thought it over and softened up about it."

"Nick, time is important to me. It grows shorter by the day."

"Your doctors say you are doing fine. Let's wait a few weeks—Christmas is coming and maybe the holidays will change her mind. I'll talk to her again sometime," Nick said, astounded at the words coming out of his mouth. He didn't want to argue with Grace Wayland again, but his sympathy went out to his dad. "I'll try again soon. We won't give up." When he stood, Eli crossed the room.

"I don't want to give up. This is my grandson. I'm sticking to what I want, to know him and give him our family name."

Nick nodded. "I tried, Dad. I better go. I have an eleven-o'clock appointment. I'll let myself out."

On his way out, Nick checked in with the nurse and the staff, then left. Relieved to have broken the news to his dad, he wondered whether his dad would give up. Nick didn't want to argue further with Grace. With a little time maybe his dad's feelings about the baby would cool, although Nick knew that was probably wishful thinking. His dad was like a dog with a bone over something he wanted and couldn't have. He would go after it and hang on like crazy.

Nick shifted his thoughts to business, running over the information he had been given for a morning appointment to discuss a land acquisition in the Dakotas. Wrapped in thoughts about business, he continued to the twenty-story building in downtown Dallas that housed the Rafford energy company.

Business occupied Nick for the rest of the day until late afternoon, when his direct line rang and he saw it was a call from his dad.

"I knew it," he said under his breath, wondering what scheme his father had hatched during the day to pressure Grace about the baby. His father wouldn't discuss it over the phone, so Nick promised to drive out and see him after work.

He replaced the receiver and spent another hour working before closing up.

As he walked through his secretary's station he smiled. "See you tomorrow, Jeananne."

"Have a good evening," she answered.

"Thanks, I will," he said as he left, wondering if his father was going to make another plea that would mean dealing with Grace. He couldn't imagine any other reason for the request to drive out and see him again. They went months without seeing each other. Twice in one day had to mean something was brewing.

Nick drove through the estate, up the winding driveway past the statuary and fountains. He continued to the back, the easiest way in, greeting the staff and heading this time for his father's favorite living area.

Still in his cardigan and slippers, Eli smiled. "Thanks for coming. I want to talk further about this problem of Michael."

"I figured you did."

"Would you like to join me in a drink? I have a fine bottle of red wine."

"Sure, Dad. Let me," Nick said, crossing the room to the bar where a bottle of red wine had already been placed on the counter with two crystal glasses beside it.

He uncorked the bottle to pour the Pinot Noir.

"So how are profits this month?" Eli asked.

"Better than last month," Nick answered, picking up their drinks. "I have a land deal in North Dakota that will be good I think."

"I don't worry that you'll ever spread yourself too thin even though you do take risks."

"You recognize you have to take risks," Nick said. "I learned that from you."

"Here's to success," Eli said, lifting his glass of wine.

Nick sat in a navy wing chair facing his father and lifted his glass. "I'll gladly drink to that. So what's up?"

Eli smiled. "I'm aware how persuasive you can be when you want to be. I'm going to do a little arm-twisting myself. Nick, I want my grandbaby in my life. I'm counting on you to see to it that my wish is granted."

"I've tried. With Bart signing away his rights and declaring that he wanted nothing to do with the baby, there's little I can do."

"You made tentative overtures about my seeing Michael. I want Michael legally my grandson and to have my name. I intend to get what I want."

Now Eli sounded like himself and not a frail, aging man. Nick wondered where the conversation was going and what his dad had in mind.

"I talked to my lawyer today. Harvey came out to the house after lunch. I hate to do this, Nick, but I don't think you're taking me seriously or are convinced about how much I want my grandson in my life."

"Wrong. I'm definitely taking you seriously," Nick said as he braced for another odious assignment.

"Well, you will now. As of this afternoon, I have two new wills. One leaves the bulk of my estate, the houses, my possessions to you with a trust for Michael and five million when he reaches twenty-one. The other will leaves my sizable fortune to charity with the exception of this house and one million to you."

"You're cutting me out of your will," Nick said, shocked and staring at his father.

"I hope not. I don't want to have to use that will. If you get Grace Wayland to agree to allowing me to legally have Michael declared a Rafford and to let me know him, I will shred that will and you will get the bulk of everything I own. Otherwise, Nick, your inheritance is cut. You won't starve or be broke—you're a multimillionaire already—but I'm worth a lot and I'm sure this will give you an incentive."

"Damn it, Dad, I can't move that woman to do what she doesn't want to do or legally doesn't have to do," Nick said. He was barely hanging on to his temper, exasperated with his father's unreasonable demands.

Eli smiled. "Think about it. You have monumental achievements. Women like you, Nick. I can count on you. Make no mistake though, I mean what I say. Harvey has the wills and my instructions."

"So exactly what do I have to get her to agree to? Let me get this clear. You want more than a visit with the baby."

"I want him in the family. I want her to willingly go to court with us and give him the Rafford name."

"Damn it," Nick said. There was no point in arguing and the sooner he got out of his father's presence, the less likely they were to get into a real battle of wills. He stood. "Under the circumstances, I better start making plans. I'll think over what you want," he said, glancing at his watch. "I have to go, Dad. I'll see what I can do."

"I'm sure of your success, Nick." Eli raised his glass in the gesture of a toast.

"You haven't met Grace Wayland. She has strong feelings about our family."

"You'll convince her otherwise. I've never seen the woman you couldn't wrap around your little finger."

Nick shook his head and left. As he drove to his condo, he mulled over the turn in his life. His father meant what he'd said. Nick knew it was no idle threat. And he didn't want to toss away a fortune and give up. Not without a fight.

The problem loomed a full-scale battle. Grace hadn't wanted to let his dad see the baby, much less actually let him become part of the family.

Nick thought of her green eyes flashing with fire. The

prospect of seeing her again was two-edged. He hadn't been able to get her out of his mind since they met. On the other hand, he had little relish for the struggle to win her over. He had tried reasoning with her. Now he'd just have to try charming her.

He concentrated on driving while he began to map out his next move.

Grace ran over the bookings for the coming week. Christmas was approaching and she had a long list of parties. She glanced up to see her assistant.

"Nick Rafford is here," Jada announced.

"Tell him to come in," Grace said. "I'll get this over with quickly."

"I don't think I'd be in a rush," Jada said, smiling.

Grace was certain he would try to talk her into yielding on her refusal to meet with his father. She'd hated the jump in her pulse when he had called for this appointment. She was just as annoyed now that she experienced a tingling awareness of him as well as being unable to avoid thinking about how she looked. And she had talked too long to him today on the phone. What should have been a five-minute call had turned into half an hour before she realized how much time she was spending.

While she placed papers in a file cabinet, Jada announced Nick.

"Grace, here's Nick Rafford."

Hoping she didn't reveal the physical reaction, the hitch in her breathing at the sight of him, she motioned toward a chair. He was the most handsome man she had ever known. "Please have a seat."

"Thanks. Ever the businesswoman," Nick said, smiling with a flash of white teeth that were as flawless and winning as the rest of his appearance. As before, his dark eyes kept her spellbound until she realized she was gazing back, with silence spreading thickly between them.

"So what brings you to my office?" she asked, trying to be brisk and cut the breathlessness from her voice. How could the man stir such a reaction by nothing more than his presence? She was amazed by his effect on her. Men didn't set her heart racing and make her insides tingly. Nick had never flirted with her and they barely knew each other, yet her response to the sight of him was unmistakable. Worse, he heightened her consciousness of herself, her plain navy skirt and shirt, the shortness of the skirt that didn't reach her knees. Again she was mindful of her drab, simple office, something she seldom had given a thought about until Nick.

"I assume this is your busiest time of the year, unless June weddings bump Christmas to second place," he said. He looked relaxed as if in total command of the situation in spite of having been soundly dismissed in their last meeting.

"Good guess. This is the busiest season and June is second."

"That's what I figured. The last time I saw you I made my case. I'm here on a different errand. This time I want to drop family matters. I'm doing what I would have done if we'd met under different circumstances. Namely, I'd like to take you to dinner—strictly a man and a beautiful woman he would like to know better. Just an evening out with nothing else going on for a few hours."

.   She laughed. "You're doing this to soften me up for another argument about Michael."

Amusement lit his dark eyes and heightened his already overwhelming appeal. "Maybe, but that isn't my intention for this one night. You're an attractive woman," he said quietly, causing her more palpitations. "You're single. I want to take you out. Are you free tonight?"

She wanted to answer yes, accept his invitation and

have an exciting night with a handsome man who lit fires
in her. At the same time, common sense screamed to avoid
any close contact with him. He wanted her most precious
possession—Michael.

Nick Rafford was accustomed to winning big battles,
acquiring what he wanted when pitted against more formidable
opponents than a single woman guardian. She had no illusions
about his invitation, but that didn't take away the temptation
to accept.

"I can see the wheels turning. Stop worrying about my
motives." He leaned forward and picked up her hand, placing
his thumb on her wrist. "Your pulse is racing, as is mine." His
strong fingers were warm, a steady, light pressure that made
her heart beat faster. His brooding dark eyes held a promise
of sensuality. "Say yes, Grace," he coaxed in a husky voice.
"I'll take you home tonight any time you want. Let's have a
few hours together. The night promises fireworks. How about
I pick you up around seven?"

"Yes," she whispered, "if my aunt is free to keep Michael.
I'll contact her," she said, retrieving her phone from a pocket.
When Grace broke the connection, she nodded. "I'm free.
I expect you to keep your promise of taking me home if I
ask."

"I swear. I've never gone against a woman's wishes
concerning a relationship."

"You can't describe dinner together as a 'relationship.' I'm
barely acquainted with you," she said, aware now his thumb
traced lightly back and forth on her wrist and her palm, faint
strokes that wreaked more havoc.

"I gave you a truthful reply to your statement. Hopefully,
a reassuring one."

"This is one of the nights this month that I have open. There
aren't too many of them." When she withdrew her wrist and

stood, he came to his feet. "Speaking of business, I should get back to work," she said.

Once again she thought she detected amusement in his torrid gaze. He stood close enough for her to notice his inviting aftershave. Without thinking, she looked at his mouth. Would they kiss tonight? She could feel the heat rise in her cheeks at the prospect of Nick's kiss. It had been a long time since she had gone out with anyone.

"Selfishly, I'm glad there's no man in your life right now."

"There isn't and hasn't been for a while. For the past seven months, I've been too busy with Michael. Before that, for years my time has gone to learning the catering business and then starting up my own."

"Sounds as if you're overdue for a night on the town. Let's make it a bigger deal and start at six. Will that be too soon?"

Her mind raced, because six would mean closing early. Yet how long had it been since she had gone out for the evening other than to cater? A few hours with a handsome, sexy man. No diapers, no responsibilities, no rushing to keep a party running smoothly. Anticipation bubbled in her.

"Six will be fine."

"See you then," he said, and left.

As she went back to the task at hand, her mind kept returning to Nick. Was she making a huge mistake by getting better acquainted with him?

She went to find Jada. "Since we don't have anything booked tonight, I accepted Nick's dinner offer."

Jada squealed with delight and wrung her hands in glee. "Sweet! You're going out with Nick Rafford! He is the handsomest man I've ever seen! How awesome!" Her ponytail bounced as she danced.

"Jada, he's Michael's uncle. He probably has ulterior motives."

Jada waved her hands in the air. "Of course he doesn't. And if he does, you'll be able to cope. Go seduce him and marry him."

Grace had to laugh. "I barely know him. Besides, the man has publicly been quoted as a confirmed bachelor and his father had multiple marriages. Also—marry Michael's uncle?"

"A legal guardian is not a blood relative. You certainly aren't a blood relation even though you're the only mother Michael knows."

"I'm having dinner for the first—and maybe last—time with Nick. What I came to tell you is that he wants to go early, so about two let's close up and get out of here. Everything is set for tomorrow night, isn't it?"

"Yes, and if he asks you out again, I can handle the Whitman party just fine. We have our help ready and I can take care of the Lansing party."

"I'm certain you can, but I'll be around. He hasn't asked me out tomorrow night."

"He will," Jada said with a grin. "I'm just sure he will."

Grace shook her head. "I'm going back to my office. I've had as much enthusiasm as I can stand," she said, wondering what Jada would be like when she fell in love.

By two the office was closed and Grace drove to her aunt's to see Michael for a while before going home. She was thankful she wouldn't have to hear another person bubbling over her dinner date—her aunt would do no such thing.

She gave Clara a hug and then turned to pick up Michael as he stretched out his arms and cooed, babbling "Ma-ma."

He smelled of baby powder and formula as she hugged him and he clung to her. He was warm and soft, cooing and babbling. She was sure she loved him more each day that passed. She looked beyond him at her aunt. "You're sure about tonight?"

"Absolutely. Are you certain about going out with Nick? If they try to take Michael from you, I wouldn't be able to stand it. He's a grandson to me."

"Don't worry. Do what I do. Remind yourself that I have the papers Bart Rafford signed giving up Michael. I have the letter he gave Alicia, and the attorney has Bart's recorded testimony giving up his rights to his son. I have Alicia's will where her wishes for Michael are clear."

"Thank goodness she lived several weeks, long enough for the arrangements to take place."

"I think she was hanging on partially because of settling who cared for Michael," Grace said. She sat on the floor and put Michael down to play with him. "I'll be here for about an hour if you want to do anything."

"I might run to the neighborhood grocery. I won't be gone long," Clara said.

"Take your time. Michael and I will have fun," Grace replied, clapping her hands and then putting Michael's tiny hands together.

She continued to play with the baby after Clara's return until Clara finally pointed to the clock. "Grace, I hate to interrupt, but soon Michael will be getting hungry and you're going to have to go home to change now if you want to be on time."

"I have plenty of time," Grace said, getting to her feet and picking up Michael. She talked to him as she carried him with her to the door and then turned to hand him to Clara.

"Aunt Clara, are you sure you want him tonight?"

"Yes, I am. He's a sweet baby and easy to have. You don't have many nights out for anything that's just fun for you. You go enjoy yourself, but be careful. The Raffords are powerful, ruthless men with money and resources."

"I'll be careful. He promised just an outing with no talk about Michael or families."

"Talk is easy and Nick Rafford is accustomed to manipulating people far more experienced than you are."

"I'll be careful, I promise," Grace said as she left.

At her apartment she showered and dressed in a wine-colored dress with a plunging vee neck and long sleeves. She brushed her hair up, looping and pinning it with a few free strands. Finally she stepped into high-heeled pumps and did a brief inspection in the chipped mirror. "You're out of your league," she said to herself, thinking of Nick. Her gaze fell to Michael's framed picture on a table and she picked it up. "I love you," she whispered. "I don't want to lose you." She kissed the picture lightly, the glass cold against her lips and then she retrieved a tissue to wipe off the slight smudge.

When the doorbell rang, she picked up her coat and purse, glancing around the empty room that seemed a haven. With her pulse quickening, she went to meet Nick.

Three

Nick's smile melted her fears and reluctance. On her doorstep beneath the porch light stood over six feet of handsome male, impeccably dressed in a charcoal suit that had likely cost more than her last month's profits. Even white teeth, creases bracketing his sensual lips, a seductive approval in his gaze—all enticed. Packaged for seduction, he radiated confidence that increased his physical appeal. Behind him a sleek black limo waited.

Small wonder she was weak-kneed and shaken, hot and definitely bothered. As well as speechless.

"You look gorgeous," he said with warmth in his dark brown eyes.

"Thank you. You appear quite handsome yourself, but I'm sure you're accustomed to hearing that."

"This is the first time I've heard you say it. I'll admit, I'm pleased," he said. "Do you want to tell your aunt and Michael goodbye?"

"Michael is at Aunt Clara's house," Grace said, wondering if he had planned on getting to see Michael tonight, but it was his father who wanted to meet Michael. She couldn't imagine that Nick cared in the least about a baby nephew.

"In that case, are you ready for a night out?"

"Yes, I am," she answered truthfully, smiling at him. He touched her cheek lightly with his forefinger.

"That's better. I haven't seen many smiles—something I intend to change tonight."

"The issues between us are not conducive to merriment."

"That definitely has to change. Let's get started."

She nodded and slipped into her worn black coat, closing the door behind her. A cold wind whipped her and she pulled her coat collar closer. "It's dark so early now," she remarked, shivering in the cold.

"You'll be warm in a second."

"I've never ridden in a limo, a fact that I'm certain doesn't surprise you. While you, on the other hand, have ridden in them since before you can remember."

A chauffeur opened the door and she climbed inside the luxurious interior, thinking it was an enormous waste of space for just two of them. While she noticed the lavish conveniences, her attention shifted to Nick. He sat near her, partially turning to face her and stretching his arm along the seat. Wind had caught a lock of his midnight hair and blown it over his forehead, heightening his appeal.

"You could live in here," she observed, only half aware of what she said because her attention was on Nick. "With the exception of a bed and bath, this is a mobile home."

His amused expression made her realize how inexperienced she must sound. "I can see why you're not in a topcoat," she continued. "Your limo is toasty warm." She slipped out of her coat and had started to pull it around her shoulders until Nick took over the task. His warm fingers brushed her nape, creating sizzles. "So tell me about this life of yours, Nick. It's vastly removed from mine."

"Not unlike your own life, except I'm not starting up a business. We both work to accomplish our goals," he said, his eyes taking leisurely inventory of her features, pausing on her mouth with a directness that caused her lips to part as she inhaled quickly. "We make decisions. We deal with people and accounting." He continued his bland list while his satisfied expression brought heat to her cheeks. He could see the effect he was having with nothing except a sensual visual survey. "We're both single. We both live in Dallas."

"You make it sound plain and simple, but it's not. I've seen local papers and magazines," she said, hoping she gave a sensible reply. She felt trapped in a web of sensuality that he spun effortlessly. Trying to focus her attention solely on their conversation and break his spell, she looked away.

"I go to parties. I imagine you do, too," he continued.

She smiled at him. "When I do, I don't get my picture taken."

"Something I can forgo," he stated.

She glanced out the window as they drove through downtown Dallas, where holiday lights multiplied the feeling of a fantasy evening.

"So, Grace, what do you want in life? Dallas's largest catering business? A chain? What's your ultimate goal?"

"I want my own successful restaurant or restaurants," she said, sharing her ambition with him and surprised at how well he could convey an illusion of intense interest in her life, something that cajoled information from her. "Since my first job I've worked in restaurants. I started with my aunt and uncle, who had a modest restaurant that was reasonably successful. When Uncle Pete died, Aunt Clara sold the restaurant and retired." Grace was aware as she talked that she had Nick's undivided attention. His steady gaze gave her the sense that he was spellbound by every word she said. She could see that such concentration would cause people to reveal more to him.

"A restaurant is open six or seven days a week, requiring long hours and demanding work, I would imagine."

"So how many hours a week do you put in?" she asked, suspecting he worked longer hours often.

He smiled. "You make your point. Now what do you do for recreation?"

"Now my pleasure is in taking care of and playing with Michael. He's a delight. Compared to yours, my life is simple. While we have things in common, we live in different worlds. I don't ride in limos and jet off to Europe."

"From the first, you've surprised me. I expected someone entirely different."

"Maybe you had preconceived notions about Alicia as well as me. While you, on the other hand, filled my expectations completely."

"Ouch. That means predictable and a few other undesirable descriptions."

"Not necessarily. I had the advantage of hearing beforehand about you from the media," she said.

"Don't believe the tabloids. Except the confirmed-bachelor part. My father has married enough to scare me from that forever."

"I'm sure." Glancing outside, she gave him a questioning look. "Where are we going?"

"Since you haven't had a night out in a long time, I tried to think of something special. We're taking my plane to Houston, where we'll board my yacht. When you're ready, we'll fly back the same way."

"Your yacht," she echoed, unable to believe she was headed for the experience he outlined. An evening on a yacht in the Gulf with a handsome multimillionaire. How had she tumbled so abruptly into a magical night that she would never forget in her entire life? Her excitement soared over the prospects. "You meant what you said when you told me something special," she remarked. Her anticipation caused her to flash him an eager smile.

"Ah, your smile—that makes my efforts worthwhile. Regrettably we got started in a manner that prevented many smiles from either of us," he said softly. "You have a smile that should get you the world," he added, his eyes warm.

"I think your flattery probably makes more gains than my smiles have," she answered lightly, aware they were treading on dangerous ground by flirting.

"I figured you would have a sitter for Michael and have to get home tonight."

"I definitely have to get home tonight," she said quickly, wondering if seduction was in his planned schedule. He grinned, an infectious, disarming grin that caused the temperature in the limo to climb.

"I'll get you home whenever you're ready to leave. Both flights are short. Sometime we can do something more spectacular and take a little longer."

"You're so certain we'll be friends despite having a life-changing disagreement between us."

"We'll see about that 'disagreement,' but not tonight. Tonight is your special night to get away from the demands of caring for a baby. No matter how adorable he is, a night out is long overdue."

She watched as they took the road for the airport. In minutes they drove past hangars across the tarmac and stopped. Nick went ahead, turning to offer his hand, holding hers as she stepped down.

Another cold wind struck her. Nick held her coat while she slipped her arms into it and pulled it close. He took her arm and they hurried to the waiting jet. Even through her coat, his firm touch stirred electricity.

She boarded another luxurious conveyance. Nick sat in a chair only a few feet from her. His raven hair, ruffled by wind, tumbled over his forehead. Watching him rake his fingers through his hair, she had visions of running her own fingers through the thick, wavy strands. The more tousled he looked, the more his appeal heightened. How easily he evoked a lusty reaction in her. Annoyed with herself, she couldn't resist watching as dark hairs sprang away from his hand.

In seconds she was buckled into the comfortable seat, facing Nick, her coat taken by an attendant who had also asked for her drink order.

Offered various cocktails and wine, she had chosen a glass of Pinot Grigio when she would have preferred a cup of steaming coffee, but that had not been in the offering. True to what Nick had predicted, she warmed rapidly and by the time they were airborne and the myriad lights of Dallas twinkled below, her chill had vanished.

"You were telling me about your life until our conversation was interrupted," he reminded her.

"I've told you what my big goals are. What are yours?" she asked, hoping to direct their conversation to his past. "I can't imagine what you want when you already have everything."

"No one has everything. I have goals—to increase business, to be a success at it."

"I'd guess there's something in your life that you want that's far more specific. What drives you, Nick?" she asked, aware that when she said his name it seemed more personal than with anyone else she ever talked to.

She caught a fleeting expression of something she couldn't define—surprise? Amusement? "Perhaps you don't want to tell me," she added quickly, unaccustomed to prying into people's lives.

"I'll answer any question you ask," he said. The words couldn't hold a double entendre, but they achieved that result with her anyway.

"I want to become a billionaire," he answered with a flat tone that made her realize this was important and a goal that surprised her. "Actually, I'd like to make more than my dad has. Maybe that's competitive. If so, it's the way he raised me to be."

They paused in the conversation as the attendant returned with a bottle of wine, uncorked it and let Nick give his approval before pouring the pale wine and serving it. As soon as they were alone, Nick leaned closer and lifted his glass.

"Here's to a fabulous escape for you."

"I'll toast that one," she replied, touching his glass lightly with her own. Her gaze was captured again by Nick's as they both raised their glasses for a sip. In midnight depths she detected a look that conveyed unmistakably that before this evening ended, he would kiss her. Her pulse jumped. The prospect heated her and she wanted him to. If he reached for her this moment, she would go into his embrace eagerly.

As if he discerned her thoughts, his gaze became heavy lidded, erotic.

Realizing where they were heading, she made an effort to end the spell, sipping her wine and looking away. Mentally, she searched for the broken threads of their conversation to pick up where they stopped. "You were telling me your goal, which I cannot fathom."

"It seems simple to me," he replied, leaning back again.

"You're already a multimillionaire. It boggles my mind to have so much wealth and strive to obtain more."

"Actually the money is not the exciting part. The battle to *acquire* riches, as well as manage a fortune so what you have makes more, feeds my ambition."

"You need a challenge," she said, realizing what motivated

him. Fear emerged from the discovery, because Eli's goal concerning Michael and her rejection pitted Nick against her in an unmistakable contest.

"Life's more interesting when fighting for something and infinitely more satisfying when I win."

"Perhaps that's the main part. You plan to win."

"Absolutely. Who plans to fail?" he asked, stretching out long legs that were only inches from touching her.

"Now you worry me. That drive definitely applies to your mission for your father," she stated solemnly.

Instantly Nick straightened and placed his hands on the arms of her chair, hemming her in and commanding her total attention. His face was only inches away and she could barely breathe.

"Not necessarily. Tonight, absolutely not. I talked about my life goal. I didn't have a thought in my head about my father. While we're together, my entire aim is to get to know an enticing woman," he added, lowering his voice, his expression as warm as a caress, making her insides jelly.

"All right, Nick," she whispered. "I believe you." She could not avoid shifting her gaze to his mouth. She wanted to kiss him. Mindful that was an unequivocal path to disaster, she longed to press her lips to his.

Their pilot announced an approach to Hobby in Houston, breaking the spell.

Nick flicked a knowing glance at her as he leaned away.

She gulped air into her empty lungs. He was a spellbinder. Effortlessly, he had crumbled her resistance and she reminded herself to get a better grip on her responses.

The minute they emerged from the plane, she shed her coat and realized why Nick hadn't worn a topcoat. Warm coastal air enveloped her and she smiled in delight. "Ah, this is grand," she said.

"Excellent. I want the entire evening to be grand," Nick said, and she smiled at him.

They boarded the chopper that whisked them to his luxurious white yacht floating on dark water. The magical atmosphere increased, Nick weaving a spell that could mesmerize her completely.

After meeting the captain and part of the crew, Nick held her arm. "Let's go to the top deck for a drink and we'll dine. Afterward I'll give you a tour."

"Sounds perfect," she said.

They rode in a glass elevator that revealed a view of a sweeping staircase, floors beautifully outfitted and enormous pots of exotic plants. When the doors opened, she stepped onto a deck that increased her sense of unreality. A small band played and she saw a table set, centered with a crystal vase holding bird of paradise blooms tucked between white orchids and plumerias.

"Nick, it's paradise here. Warm weather, a yacht, the lights reflecting on the water. The docks and coastline are decorated for the holidays—various colored lights as if this is part of a colossal party," she said, turning to smile at him.

"I'm slipping," he said. "Water, flowers, yacht, lights—I was in hopes I'd be in that list somewhere."

Feeling giddy, she laughed. "You, sir, are the pièce de résistance," she admitted, tossing caution overboard.

"That's infinitely better," Nick stated, turning her and taking her into his arms to dance to the ballad the band played.

Startled, she followed his lead. In spite of the slight space between them, she detected his inviting aftershave. Through the fine wool of his suit jacket and his shirt, she felt the warmth of his arm. His hand holding hers heightened her sensory reaction.

"I'm in a dream tonight. You've succeeded beyond my

wildest hopes. I never guessed I'd spend an evening like this."

"I'm more than pleased and if you think you're the only person having a great time, you're wrong."

She smiled. "For a few hours, there is no tomorrow and no routine life," she said. "Only paradise and a handsome charmer," she admitted, conscious she played with fire. Raging fire. Even so, she refused to allow caution to reemerge.

The music ended and Nick led her to their table. "I have champagne."

"It has to be followed by coffee when we eat. I'm not into wine and champagne and magic."

He smiled as he opened the champagne with a pop and poured it into slender flutes. He offered the bubbling drink.

"Nick, this yacht is moving," she said, startled by the realization that they were sailing.

"Don't be alarmed. We're traveling only a short distance along the shoreline and then circling back. I thought you'd enjoy seeing the lights and it would be more pleasurable than remaining anchored."

The fleeting question arose: could she trust him and accept what he promised?

As if he discerned her thoughts, he spoke. "I promised we'd go back whenever you want. If you're uneasy, we can return now and eat at one of the restaurants," he said, and she felt foolish.

"I just don't know you very well."

"Say the word and we'll return right now."

She shook her head. "Thanks, but no. I'm just unaccustomed to getaways like this."

"Text your aunt, tell her where you are," he said. "I think you'll feel better. I'll talk to the band." He walked away and, losing her qualms, she followed his suggestion, grateful that he had made it.

When she finished the message, she took her drink to the rail. After a few minutes Nick joined her.

"Feel better now?" Without waiting for her answer, he continued, "Is everything all right at home?"

"Yes. Michael is sleeping and my aunt is getting ready to watch her favorite show."

They stood, chatting about nothing in particular and watching lights along the shore slip past until she realized they were moving slightly away from land, angling toward the turn he'd indicated.

During dinner, while each course was lavish, culminating in succulent lobster, her appetite was diminished by the charisma generated by Nick. "I haven't relaxed and enjoyed myself like this in months," she remarked, looking at him and smiling. "Actually, in this manner, never. I know you know how to relax. You have a reputation in the media."

"In the tabloids. I hope you aren't relying on those for your info about me."

"Definitely not! I'm relying on my own observations. My friend Alicia never mentioned you. I don't think she ever met you."

"No. In hindsight, I might have been better off if I had met her."

"You probably wouldn't believe me if I told you she hadn't had many relationships with men. She was in love with a guy right after high school. That lasted a year. Then there were a couple more. She ran around with friends who were male, but nothing serious, nor did she sleep with them."

"You sound as certain as if you were talking about yourself."

"I am. We grew up together in bad circumstances. Both our families were poor. Worse, her father died when she was seven. Mine died when I was eleven. Alicia and I were as close as sisters, in fact, closer than I am to my own sisters. And she only had one brother who was killed three years ago. Alicia and I shared our hopes and disappointments. When she met your brother, he swept her off her feet. His money impressed her. She also liked him."

"Money impresses a lot of women. Women liked my older brother and vice versa. No problem there."

"I'm sure you receive the same reactions."

"I didn't from you," he reminded her. "That's where you threw me a curve. Principle before money? I never expected that response when I talked to you Monday morning."

"Michael is more important than money to me. I've spent nearly my whole life without money."

"That's why you should have been so awed and willing," Nick remarked.

"No. Michael is my son now," Grace replied, hoping to reinforce her position. "I took Michael home from the hospital after he was released from neonatal intensive care. His premature birth was terrifying. Now it would scare me more because I love him so much and feel as if he's my baby."

"He's actually my brother's baby—at least according to what I've been told."

"He is definitely your brother's child," she stated, realizing Nick's food was as forgotten as her own. "I knew my friend almost as well as I know myself. I've told you there were no other men in her life when she met your brother. Actually, Michael looks as if he's your son. When you see Michael, you'll know your brother was his father."

Nick's eyes narrowed. "We bear a resemblance? I'd never thought of that. I look like my father, so that means Michael might. That isn't something you can fabricate."

"Or exaggerate. I'm sure you'll eventually see for yourself. He looks like your son. No one could possibly disagree."

Nick gazed into space and she wondered why the discovery had silenced him. Had he figured this was another man's baby and dismissed his father's wishes? She didn't know what ran through Nick's mind, but the news that he and Michael bore a strong family resemblance troubled Nick.

He frowned slightly as he turned back to her. "Michael doesn't look like Bart? Did you ever meet Bart?"

"No, I didn't, but I saw a snapshot of him. I don't think Michael resembles Bart. Bart had hazel eyes, brown hair."

"Bart and I are actually half brothers. We had different mothers."

"That's something I didn't know."

"Bart and I had our own lives and were busy. Time slips away." Nick lapsed into silence again. A short while later he looked at her plate.

"Neither of us is eating. There's a great dessert."

"I'll pass, although everything is delicious."

"We can have the dessert later. C'mon, and I'll give you that tour," Nick said, standing and coming to take her arm.

As he showed her the upper decks, Nick kept the conversation on ordinary events, shared interests in movies and books. When he led her into his master suite, her senses spiked and her nerves became raw. She looked at the luxurious burnished-wood built-in furniture, rich brown leather upholstery, and a wide king-size bed covered in satin.

"Here's where I sleep when I stay on board," Nick said. His voice lowered, developing a husky note. Again his words were harmless, but his tone, his gaze when she looked up at him, his hand lightly on her arm—all combined to have her picture herself lying on his bed in his embrace.

When he turned her to face him, her heart thudded. His hand on her arm was one more casual contact that should have been meaningless but instead was sizzling. She didn't want this fiery attraction that kept her breathless with him, yet there was no denying it. She wanted his kiss, could actually feel herself lean slightly toward him. His dark eyes warmed, his lids partially closing as he gazed at her mouth. She gathered her wits and her will.

"Nick, we should go back. Maybe dance now," she whispered, making an effort to turn away. Her heartbeat galloped in anticipation. Before the evening was over they would kiss and that knowledge played havoc with her nerves. Desire heightened, plaguing her.

"If that's what you want," he said.

They returned to the upper deck, where he drew her into his arms to dance, holding her lightly, gazing at her as they moved together in complete unison.

Hours later, as they stood talking quietly at the rail, she turned to him. "This is a bewitching night, Nick. You shouldn't make it so unforgettable and enticing."

"Why not? We can have a life separate from the problems caused by my father."

"Actually, I don't think we can," she said. "And it's time to start back home."

"Whatever you want," he said, smiling at her as they left the rail.

Within the hour they were airborne and Nick was entertaining her with more tales from his past.

It was almost three in the morning when his limo stopped at her apartment complex and Nick walked her to the door. "Give me your key and let me open the door."

Wordlessly, she handed over the key. He pushed open the door and held it for her to enter, following her inside and closing the door while she cut off the alarm. She turned to face him.

"Thank you, Nick. The evening was a dream come true—a night I'll remember for a very long time."

"It's not over yet," he said in a husky voice, slipping an arm around her waist and drawing her closer. At his hungry look, she glanced at his sensuous mouth, wanting to step into his embrace and kiss him, to be kissed. Yet once she did, her life might not ever be the same.

"Nick, this is dangerous, foolish," she whispered.

"Shh, it's only a kiss. It's meaningless—a goodbye, a touch. A kiss won't change our lives or the future."

"You are so sure of yourself," she said quietly, the tension growing between them. The warning inside grew dimmer. She couldn't look away from Nick's dark eyes, couldn't move away from him. Could he hear her heart pounding? Or feel her pulse racing?

Lightly, his fingers drifted along her throat, then up to her ear and in her hair while his arm tightened around her waist, drawing her closer.

"Nick, we shouldn't," she said, but her protest was weak, more of an invitation. She was losing ground, succumbing to desire. She inhaled and stepped back, out of his embrace. "You're not going to charm me into giving you what you want. You wanted this night to be about getting to know each other."

"I've kept my promise. I haven't pushed you about Michael."

"You did what you promised," she acknowledged. "I had a wonderful time, but now you need to go."

He gazed at her in silence and she could see the craving burning in the depths of his eyes. He nodded. "I'll take you to lunch Tuesday and we can talk."

He turned and was gone, the door closing quietly behind him.

She stared at the door. Every inch of her yearned to call him back, to step into his embrace and kiss. Kisses that she suspected would be as spellbinding as the entire evening had been. Desire scalded her. She wanted him with a hunger she wouldn't have believed possible.

She had done the right thing by keeping a distance between

them. Then why was it so unsatisfactory and why did she long to be in his arms?

Sleep was lost for most of the remainder of the night. The time with Nick replayed in her mind while longing heightened instead of diminishing. She had to forget Nick, go on with her life, keep Michael safe from the Raffords, but it was difficult to think of never seeing Nick again. Lunch Tuesday. He wanted to talk about Michael. She could refuse, stop this before it went any further. Nick's dark brown eyes and the way he had held her when they danced tormented her until she finally drifted to sleep and dreamed about kissing Nick.

Four

At home Nick swam laps in his pool, trying to cool his raging libido. He ached to kiss Grace, too aware she had wanted to kiss. Her green eyes had conveyed lust and she had come close to succumbing. He was determined to win her over. Too much rested on the outcome of his dealings with her. He was accustomed to getting what he wanted and he intended to with Grace.

Meanwhile, he wanted her with an urgency that surprised him. He thought about her constantly and he couldn't recall doing that with any other woman.

Grace was different. Why? Was it solely the money that he would win or lose? She was a beautiful woman, but his life was filled with other entrancing women. Was it just because she was a challenge when he so seldom found a ravishing woman who resisted him?

Whatever the reason, getting his inheritance was essential. Tuesday, he intended to walk away from that appointment with a promise from her to let his dad meet Michael. With his father's health so frail, time was of the essence.

She had to move lunch Tuesday to two o'clock. She had spent the early hours getting dressed, finally selecting a simple navy suit and silk blouse. Then she had spent the rest of the morning reminding herself to resist whatever Nick asked.

Nick insisted on picking her up at her office, so she waited at the door. When Grace saw his black sports car approach, she stepped outside, hoping she hid her own feelings, because her racing pulse and butterflies in her stomach were unwanted. Adding to her flutters, Jada had been bubbly the entire morning over the lunch appointment. With a deep breath, Grace approached the curb.

When he stepped out to open the door for her, she had another jump in her pulse at the sight of him. Lunch in the middle of the day on a Tuesday shouldn't be filled with magic in a romantic surrounding. She hoped to be practical and firm, and resist whatever he suggested, because this meeting was clearly an effort to get what he wanted from her.

"Hi," he said, the gleam in his brown eyes causing a gush of warmth. "Busy day?" he asked.

"Very. Hopefully the afternoon will be quieter. Thanks again for a Friday night that was relaxing and memorable. It was great to get away a few hours."

He flashed another smile. "For a moment there I hoped the reason was personal, not merely to get out for a few hours. We proved we don't have to battle constantly. I want to find some common ground."

"Common ground where Michael's future is concerned is entirely different. You can't undo the damage your brother did. Your family had every chance. We've been over that," she said, resentment curling sourly.

He drove to a popular place, where they hurried in the

brisk, cool wind from his car into a restaurant that had grown quiet when the noon crowd had thinned. Near a fireplace that contained the last glowing embers from a fire, Nick sat across from her. Today he was in a brown sweater over a white shirt, looking casual, handsome and exciting.

After ordering, he smiled at her. "You look great. Very efficient, very businesslike, so desirable."

"Thank you, but the latter is not on our agenda."

"For now, forget the argument between us. You know what I did Sunday and yesterday?"

"How could I possibly have any idea?" she asked, amused by his question.

"I spent far too much time thinking about you and Saturday night. And wanting another night out."

"Nick, we can't pursue a relationship," she said, clinging to caution while another part of her wanted to smile and agree. "Of course, I know you're trying to get me to cooperate one way or another."

"I'll admit I'm trying to win you over, but not exactly for the purpose you're thinking now. There are some personal, ulterior motives here that do not involve my father," Nick said, his voice deepening and the expression in his eyes conveying unmistakable desire.

Her breath was erratic. "Stop flirting, Nick. We have no future—with family or without family."

"That doesn't have to be. I know you enjoyed Saturday night. I want to go out again. And once more, it has nothing to do with the future or my nephew or my father. Grace, you kept me at arm's length on Saturday night. I intend to change that."

Spellbinding words, yet was it a ploy to get his way? If he seduced her, she would succumb to everything he wanted. Now was the time to resist him, to ignore her tingling, breathless reaction, turn a blind eye to his handsome looks, hold fast to rejection even though everything in her screamed to accept, flirt with him and go with the moment.

"You're a dirty fighter, Nick. You know there's a chemistry and you've emphasized the attraction."

"What man wouldn't?" he asked in a low voice. "You're beautiful, Grace. I'm a warm-blooded man and I like being with you."

His words heightened her reaction, melting animosity and caution. "Wisdom tells me to avoid a wide-eyed, heart-thumping acceptance of your offers," she whispered.

"Maybe wisdom, but nothing else."

"You know I react physically to you. We react to each other, although I suspect you have this response from a lot of women. But with me, you have a strong ulterior motive."

With his gaze locked on her he raised her hand, brushing a kiss on her palm while his thumb was on the vein in her wrist. He watched her intently. "See there," he said in a husky voice. "Your pulse is rushing. Far faster than normal. As is mine. If we were alone now, you'd be in my arms."

"Nick, stop this," she said, hearing words spoken in a tone that sounded more like an invitation than a denial.

"I want to take you out tonight, including eating together," he said. "Say yes, Grace. Your assistant has already told me she can cover the party for you because it's a small one with a client you've had before."

"You just go barreling ahead to get what you want," she said.

"You weren't discontented Saturday night. You've gone with me twice now and you're in no worse situation for spending time with me, so what's the harm in accepting? Especially when it shows that you want to accept."

She laughed. "You don't give up, do you?"

"Not with you, because you want to go with me. How's seven tonight?" He leaned closer. "We'll make it a short, early evening and do whatever you'd like to do. If I promise again no discussion about Michael and my dad, how's that? Now a yes," he said.

"Yes, against wisdom and caution."

"We have unfinished business."

"You promised—" she started to say.

"I'm not referring to Michael or Dad," he said.

Their waiter approached and Nick released her hand, watching her while green salads were placed in front of them.

Through lunch, Nick flirted and charmed and she forgot the problems for moments at a time until she would realize how much she responded to Nick. Each hour spent with him made her want to be with him even more. In spite of knowing that, she craved the excitement he brought into her life. Women could not resist him and in too many ways, she was no different from the others. She had capitulated easily to his dinner offer. She couldn't believe their time together meant anything to him except a means to get Michael. For her it was one more unforgettable evening instead of a few quiet hours playing with Michael and then spending the remaining time going over books for work. Just once more and then a firm, unyielding refusal. Could she really stick to that plan when Nick turned on the charm?

"I would like to talk about Michael *now*, though." Nick reached across the table to grip her hand again and her heart skipped a beat. His hand was warm, enveloping hers, causing havoc with her nerves.

"There really isn't anything to get to. My feelings haven't changed."

"Listen to me," Nick urged quietly. "You've been logical, not too emotional over this issue. Just come meet my dad and let him see and hold his grandson." Dark brown eyes bored into her while his thumb ran back and forth over her wrist, creating distracting flutters.

"How simple you make it sound," she said, her voice breathless, almost a whisper.

"It's harmless, Grace. My father is very ill. His heart is in bad shape and he's getting more frail. At least let him meet Michael and hold his grandson. Is that too much to ask?"

She withdrew her hand from Nick's. "You make it sound so easy, yet I always remember Alicia and her wishes."

"Alicia dealt with Bart. That's a whole different issue. Don't punish my father for stupid, cruel things my brother did."

"Your father could have stepped in."

"At the time my father knew nothing about Bart's rejection. Christmas is approaching—the season of giving. It's going to be damn bleak for my father. Bring the baby over and meet my dad and let him satisfy himself just seeing Michael. I'm not asking to take Michael or change his name or anything else right now. Just let Dad see him and hold him. Give him this, Grace."

She looked away, torn by Nick's plea and aware that she couldn't be that selfish over Michael, yet fearing the Raffords' power and Nick's ulterior motives. She thought about Michael and how much he resembled Nick. Once Eli Rafford saw the baby, he would never want to let him go because of that resemblance. To Eli, Michael would be Nick all over again. She was certain the remarkable resemblance would make a difference in Eli's attitude.

"Once your father sees Michael, he will never want to let him go."

"Grace, my father's days may be limited. He isn't well. He can't take Michael from you. This is only a meeting. I promise," Nick added quietly.

She looked into unfathomable brown eyes that told her nothing. This man had a reputation for being ruthless in business. Was she being naive, gullible and taken in by a charmer who had plotted every move to take Michael from her?

"We can make it short," Nick added.

"All right, Nick," she said, staring at him intently. There was no change in his expression, reminding her that he could hide his emotions completely.

"Thank you for agreeing. You'll see how much it means to him."

"You better keep your word."

"I've promised. Don't be so fearful. It'll be all right. My father can't take your baby and if you're worried that I'll try to talk you into marriage, I have no intention of bringing either a wife or a baby into my life. My freedom is important and, at this point, I don't care to become a daddy. I'll make the arrangements. When will you be free?"

She pulled her phone and checked her calendar. "I'm booked solid since it's getting so close to Christmas. I can turn the parties over to Jada either Thursday afternoon or Friday afternoon."

"I'll make arrangements with Dad for Thursday afternoon," Nick said.

"I should get back to the office. You've gotten everything you want, so we can go now," she said with a sharp note in her voice.

"Not everything."

As they left, she was conscious of his height, his body so close to hers and his hand on her arm. He had gotten everything he wanted, yet he had sounded reasonable in his requests. Time would tell. She prayed she had no regrets.

Nick kept the conversation light, but worries were already besieging her when they drove back to her office. He got out quickly and came around to open her door. "Thanks for lunch, I think," she added, emerging from the car.

"How's two o'clock Thursday afternoon?"

"That will be fine. Michael may fall asleep, but that's all right."

"I'll pick both of you up at your place. Thanks for this. You'll see, after you have this first visit with my dad, you won't be sorry about your decision."

"We'll see, Nick. Thanks for lunch." She turned to walk briskly away, her back tingling because she guessed Nick stood and watched her. She dreaded meeting Eli Rafford, suspecting her trepidation would only grow. Inside her office, she turned to watch Nick drive away. She hoped she was doing the right thing.

Thursday seemed eons away and then it was upon her. She left work early to get Michael ready only to find Clara had already bathed him and laid out clothes.

"He's been fed and I think he'll fall asleep soon," Clara said.

"If you'll watch him a few more minutes, I'm going to change clothes," Grace said, hugging Michael and giving him a kiss before handing him to Clara.

"Sure. Take your time. I'll get Michael dressed in his sailor suit."

Grace changed to tan slacks and a matching silk shirt, then brushed her hair and clipped it at the back of her neck. She returned to Michel's room to find him seated on a blanket, playing with his toys and cooing.

"He looks adorable," Grace said, her worries returning.

"I know this meeting was probably inevitable, but I just pray your legal rights are binding. Once this man sees his grandson, he'll want him more than ever."

"Nick insists that his dad simply wants to see Michael and hold him. Clara, I hope I'm not making the mistake of my life."

Clara frowned and looked at Michael, who was playing with a rattle and happily babbling unintelligible words. "Me, too, Grace. I know Nick Rafford has pressured you into this meeting. A visit sounds harmless, but once Eli Rafford sees his grandchild, I hope the resemblance to Nick doesn't reinforce his goal to give Michael the Rafford name. Or more. Eli Rafford may be frail, but he has the money for nannies and all kinds of help. He could try to take Michael and pay people to care for him round-the-clock." Nannies and staff would raise Michael instead of relatives. Clara shuddered while Grace's chill deepened.

"That's what I fear," Grace said. "They have the money to do as they please. I made an appointment to talk to my attorney in the morning."

"Thank heavens," Clara declared. "You can't fight the Rafford money, Grace. I'm afraid Nick Rafford is showering his attention on you for a reason."

"Hopefully, this afternoon will be only what Nick said, simply letting the grandfather see his grandson. That doesn't give Eli any rights, no matter how much he wants them."

"Just remember Alicia, what she went through and how she tried to cut them out of Michael's life. The man's son was selfish and dreadful."

"I know. It's pointless to tell you to not worry. I'll call you as soon as I get home."

As she glanced at her watch the doorbell rang. "Come meet Nick," she said, picking up Michael.

It was time.

Nick stood immobilized, one of the few times in his life he was consumed by shock. He forgot people, surroundings, his purpose in coming. His total attention was on the baby in Grace's arms—a baby who was a mirror of his own baby pictures.

Stunned, he stared into big, dark brown eyes with black lashes, a thick head of baby hair as jet-black as his own, the same shaped ears.

"Oh, my God," he whispered. "He could be mine."

Grace spoke, but her words didn't register with him.

"Bart never saw his son, did he?" Nick asked finally.

"No, he didn't, but that was his choice," Grace replied. "Nick, come inside and meet my aunt."

Nick inhaled deeply, stepping inside, unable to take his gaze from the baby, realizing instantly his father was in for a shock. It occurred to him that his father would never give up the battle now to get Michael legally into the Rafford family with the Rafford name.

"Aunt Clara, this is Nick Rafford. Nick, my aunt, Clara Wayland."

Nick turned his attention to the woman standing beside Grace. Her green eyes were glacial and her mouth was closed tightly as she nodded, making it obvious that she didn't approve of him or want Grace taking Michael to meet his dad.

"I've heard about you and your care for Michael," Nick said, smiling at her, certain the smile would not be returned.

"Michael is Grace's precious child now. He loves his mother very much."

Nick could feel the waves of dislike and anger from the woman. "I appreciate her sharing Michael today and letting my dad meet his grandson. That is going to mean the world to him."

"Michael can't possibly be that important since your family shunned him totally at birth and when his life was hanging by a thread."

"Something my dad is sorry about now," Nick said quietly, knowing she was immersed in anger with the Raffords. "Mrs.

Wayland, my father has no intention of taking Michael from Grace. Today, he wants to meet his grandson. Just see him."

"It isn't today that worries me," Clara snapped, and Grace placed her hand on her aunt's arm.

"It's all right. I'll go with Nick now. I'll call you when we get back. Thanks for your help today."

She buckled Michael into his carrier and Nick picked it up as Grace gathered Michael's bag. She brushed a kiss on her aunt's cheek. "Don't worry," she whispered.

"I'm glad to have met you," Nick said politely and left, waiting outside for Grace to join him.

"Sorry, but she's worried and upset."

"If I could be boiled in oil, she would have seen to it. Or a few other dreadful ways to get rid of me. Sorry to worry her so much. She could have joined us."

"Heaven forbid. She wouldn't want that and neither would you or your dad. Or any of us. She'll calm down if your intentions are really what you say."

"They are. Now I know why you looked so shocked when you first met me. I thought it was the hot chemistry between us, but, sadly that wasn't it at all. You were stunned by my resemblance to Michael," he said.

"Yes, I was surprised when I first saw you."

"Michael himself nails the Rafford paternity—except Michael looks as if he's my child instead of Bart's. There's no earthly reason to ask for a DNA test if we could. This baby is a Rafford through and through as far as appearance goes. He couldn't look more like my baby pictures. And I have a picture where I'm dressed in a sailor suit like the one you have on him today. That's going to jolt Dad."

"I didn't think of that. Should we go back and change?"

"No. I'm not going another round with your aunt."

Grace chuckled. "You? Scared of Aunt Clara?"

"I've faced opponents in board rooms who didn't look that hostile. I'm thankful she wasn't armed."

"Aunt Clara wouldn't hurt a fly. I'm shocked. You're intimidated by Aunt Clara."

"Don't rub it in. I'm amazed she hasn't spent every second trying to convince you not to go with me today—or the last time, for that matter." Nick glanced in the rearview mirror at Michael in the backseat. "I don't know anything about babies, but I'm guessing this is a very happy baby."

"He's a darling. He is a happy baby."

"I would be, too, if you were taking care of me," Nick said, and she smiled.

"Sorry, you don't qualify," she answered lightly.

"I think I'll let the nurse and my dad know about the family resemblance before we spring Michael on my dad. This is going to be a shock."

"And make him want Michael all the more."

Nick glanced at her. "Don't start worrying. Dad will be pleased I'm sure and I don't know if he can want to know Michael any more than he does right now. You can't imagine how pleased and grateful he is that you've agreed to this. You'll see," Nick said, keeping to himself what would occur. His father would take one look at Michael and get an account set up, get presents for Christmas and want all sorts of things that involved the baby. "Just remember my dad is elderly and doesn't work anymore, which used to take a lot of his time and attention. He has no women in his life and I'm not around that much. Michael will be his main focus. That doesn't mean he wants to take the baby from you. I promise you that. Dad never was into children or babies."

"He is now," she said, and her tone sounded sharp.

They rode quietly until passing through the gates to his father's estate.

"Do you have a home besides your condo?" she asked.

"Yes. I have a condo in Houston. I have a home in Colorado and a ranch in West Texas. I lead a relatively unpretentious life."

"It sounds as if you do," she remarked drily. "Yachts, businesses, women, houses, condos. So simple."

"Modest compared to what I could do if I wanted to."

They wound up the driveway that gave a full view of the front of the mansion and he heard Grace's intake of breath. "This is a castle. Who lives here besides your father?"

"His staff, which now includes his nurses. There are currently two who live here and they take different shifts. I detect worry in your voice."

"How can I fight this?" she said.

"Perhaps you won't have to," he declared, but the words carried a hollow ring. His dad would fight with his whole being to get this child declared a Rafford.

He hoped that when Grace saw the house and met his father, she would come to her senses and realize what Eli could do for Michael. And now, Nick thought his father would do more. The two wills plagued Nick constantly. More than ever, he felt he had to get Grace to cooperate as quickly as possible before his father got really attached to Michael.

At the moment, Nick wanted to gnash his teeth in frustration. Grace had to capitulate. He reminded himself that she had so far.

He pulled to a stop in front, wanting to take Grace through the most impressive entrance. The more awed she was, the more cooperative she might become. He pulled out his cell phone. "Just a minute, Grace. Let me talk to the nurse and maybe Dad."

He made the call, giving her time to take in her surroundings, the vast wings of the house, the massive statuary and fountains in front, the immaculate flower beds with an array of colorful winter plants.

When he finished, he put away the phone. "Well, let's go introduce Michael to his grandfather. Michael will never know the storm swirling around him."

"I hope not. And I hope I survive it."

"You will," Nick said, wondering if she could be rethinking her stand on keeping Michael out of the Rafford family.

Nick stepped out to open her door and pick up Michael. He took Grace's arm. "My dad's no ogre in spite of the wild tales about his business deals."

"I think you're talking about yourself there."

He chuckled as they crossed to the massive door. He heard the chimes and then the door swung open.

Five

As the door swung open and a butler faced them, intimidation enveloped Grace. She was certain that was the intention of Nick and his father. She couldn't imagine anyone ever reaching a point where they took this magnificence and wealth for granted. She reminded herself that Nick had been born into it.

"Good evening, Mr. Rafford. Your father is waiting." The butler glanced down at the baby in the carrier, and Grace heard his swift intake of breath, but his expression didn't change.

They stepped into a mammoth marble hallway where Nick set the baby carrier on a side table. The hall ceiling soared three floors, and an enormous crystal chandelier hung above her head. Ahead, two staircases wound up to the next level.

"I'll get Michael from his carrier now and take his jacket off," she said, busying herself. Her fingers were cold and stiff and she dreaded the meeting with Eli Rafford. She wished now she had never succumbed to Nick's charm or agreed to anything involving him, although she suspected it wouldn't have stopped Nick or his father and it might have made matters worse.

She picked up Michael, holding him close, wanting to keep him in her arms and never hand him over to Nick or his dad.

"Ready?" Nick asked, and she nodded, raising her chin and hoping she looked far more calm and self-assured than she felt.

Along the hall they passed open doors on rooms with magnificent furnishings. How could one frail man live in this mansion? She suspected the staff was huge.

He stopped in front of a closed door. "Dad's in here. Grace, I'm going to tell him we're here. I think Michael will really surprise my father and I don't want to give his heart too big a jolt."

"Of course," she said, and waited. Nick reappeared and motioned to her, taking her arm and walking her into the room.

"Grace, I want you to meet my father, Eli Rafford. And this is his nurse Megan Sayer. Dad, Megan, meet Grace Wayland and Michael."

The tall brown-eyed man standing beside a wing chair smiled at her. "Thank you for coming and bringing Michael, Miss Wayland," he said in a strong voice. He didn't look as infirm as she had envisioned from Nick's description. "I appreciate it very much."

The petite nurse standing nearby gave her a friendly smile. "He's been looking forward to this for quite a while."

As she greeted both of them, Grace crossed the room on a thick Oriental rug. "Here's Michael, Mr. Rafford," she said.

He looked at the baby and she saw his eyes narrow. "He is you," Eli said, glancing at Nick and then back to the baby. Eli sat in the chair. "That's an uncanny resemblance. He looks like your son, Nick. May I hold him, Miss Wayland?"

"Yes, of course. Please call me Grace."

"He does look like you, Nick," Megan said as she spread a baby blanket over Eli's lap and Grace walked forward to give Michael to his grandfather.

"My grandson," Eli Rafford said, and there was no mistaking the awe in his voice. "This is my grandson."

Grace noted that Eli seemed to have a firm grip on Michael, and Megan stood close at hand. Michael played with the buttons on Eli's sweater while he babbled.

"He's happy," Megan said.

"He's a wonderful baby," Grace added.

"Have a seat, Grace," Nick said. "Let's have something to drink. Want pop or a cup of hot tea or coffee?"

"I'll have hot tea," Grace replied, sitting in a chair near Eli. She handed Michael one of his toys, which he promptly began to chew.

"He's adorable," Megan said. "The resemblance to you is amazing, Nick. He could pass for your son. I'll see about your drinks," she said, crossing the room to an intercom.

"I'm trying to get used to the resemblance," Nick said, sitting across from her.

"I'm so pleased," Eli said, smiling broadly. "I don't know that much about babies. I'll let you have him back, but what a thrill this is. Would you allow me to have a photographer take a picture of Michael with Nick and me?"

"Of course," Grace replied, guessing that was probably the beginning of a lot of requests.

"I would treasure it. I can't tell you what pleasure you have given me by allowing me to get to know Michael. Nick, I can't believe this child doesn't belong to you."

"It gave me a shock to see him, too," Nick said.

As both men looked at Michael, Grace's worries deepened.

Eli's expression was the same as he might convey to a beloved relative even though he had never seen Michael before today. The wonder in Nick's eyes equally upset her. There would be no turning back now. Michael would be drawn into this family in spite of her efforts to avoid any contact. She had contemplated taking Michael and moving away, but her business was growing with repeat clientele. And from Alicia's dealings with the hostile Raffords, she had never thought they would be a problem. Now worries grew with each encounter.

"As I understand from Nick, you are in the catering business and your aunt takes care of Michael a lot of the time."

"Yes. I've been fortunate and Aunt Clara adores Michael. She has no grandchildren and she considers Michael a grandchild," Grace said, hoping to convey how much a part of her life and her aunt's Michael was.

"Nick wanted me to promise to keep this conversation simple and not intrude on your care of Michael, but I would like to offer to set up a small account that you can use for whatever you need for him."

"Dad, we agreed to avoid this today," Nick reminded his father.

"That's fine, Nick," she said quickly. "I appreciate your offer, Mr. Rafford," she said to avoid an argument. She had no intention of using Rafford money to care for Michael.

"Excellent! And you must call me Eli. I can't physically do much with a baby. I never did as much as I should have with my own sons, but there are other ways to play a part in his life. Also, I had my secretary get Michael some toys." Eli reached behind his chair to pull out a sack and hand to her. "You can give him what is appropriate now and let him have the others when the time is right."

"Thank you," she said politely, taking the sack from him to glance at each toy, finding both elaborate, expensive toys as well as simple ones. "Your secretary either knows babies or asked an expert because these are all suitable. Since Michael chews on everything, I'll wash them before I give them to him. Thank you. I'm certain he'll have fun." For a moment she thought of Alicia with a forlorn sense of loss for what her friend would miss, causing her to think again of Bart Rafford and the grief his selfishness had caused.

A staff member brought drinks and a plate of cookies that no one touched while Eli Rafford asked nonintrusive questions about Michael and her business and told her a little about his boys when they were young. Michael stretched out on the blanket with his toys and in a short time was asleep.

"Our conversation doesn't prevent his napping," Eli observed.

"He can sleep through most anything," Grace said, aware of Nick's gaze on her as they talked. Megan had left and Grace assumed she had been present to make certain her patient didn't receive too big a shock over Michael.

Grace could see the tall clock standing across the room behind Nick. It was almost two hours later when Michael began to stir. "I think it's time to take Michael home now," she said, knowing the baby would be hungry and need to be changed.

"Grace, I can't tell you what this meeting has meant to me," Eli said. "I'm so grateful. I know you have a busy schedule, but I hope you will come again and bring Michael with you."

"I'll be happy to," she said, thinking the visit had been easy and in some ways, it seemed right for Michael to be with his grandfather and for Eli Rafford to know his grandson.

"I'm delighted to meet his mother—which you are now and always will be." He extended his hand and she shook it, feeling a firm grip and looking into dark brown eyes that hid everything as much as Nick's.

Nick buckled Michael into the carrier and gathered the

sack of toys while Eli handed an envelope to Grace. "Inside you'll find the papers for the account I've opened. Everything is there, but if you have questions, feel free to call me. I have too much free time in my life now," he said. He walked to the door with them and leaned forward to brush a kiss on the top of Michael's head. He turned to Grace. "Thank you," he said.

"I'll see you again, Eli," she said, certain she couldn't possibly avoid it. Nick took her arm and they left.

In the car he glanced at her. "Thank you. That meant a lot to my father."

"Did you know he had opened an account?"

"No, I didn't, but I wasn't in the least surprised. I know my dad. He's manipulative and hell-bent on getting what he's after. He wants to know Michael. It's important to him and he thinks in terms of what he can do with money. This is his only grandson. He'll shower Michael with gifts."

"I feel as if I'm sinking in quicksand. The quicksand of the Raffords. I catered your party. I've spent an evening out with you, have gone to lunch with you, have met your father and let him meet Michael. It keeps growing, Nick, when I didn't want any part of your family, frankly."

"We're not monsters."

She noticed a muscle worked in his jaw. "No, you're not, but you both are men accustomed to getting what you want."

"Was it so bad today?" he asked.

"No, of course not, but I don't want your father's money."

"Don't turn it down. Take it. He doesn't need it and you can do something for Michael with it. Don't hang on to principles and grudges that would keep something good from Michael."

"I suppose I'm thinking of Alicia, who was closer to me than my sisters."

"Where are they?"

"Doreen works in Vegas and Tanya in Los Angeles. I haven't seen them for several years."

"While Bart and I went our separate ways, we were closer than that."

"Had your brother been half as receptive as your father, so much heartache could have been avoided and Alicia would still be alive. I can't keep from thinking about it."

"And I can't help what Bart did. Neither can my father. Bart was younger, had a different mother and, frankly, I always thought he was a spoiled brat about a lot of things. In ways we were close but we differed, too. And we looked nothing alike. I can't get used to the baby's resemblance to me. He shocks me every time I look at him. The whole world will think he's mine."

Nick drove to her apartment, carrying Michael inside. "He's fallen asleep again," Nick said, surprise in his voice.

"It was the car ride. He won't sleep long because it's past time for him to eat. I didn't want to get out a bottle at your dad's and stay to feed Michael." She glanced at Nick. "Well, you did it, Nick. Now I've been to your dad's and he's met Michael and he's definitely in Michael's life."

The minute she looked into Nick's eyes, her knees became jelly. Desire was fire in depths of brown. Her mouth went dry and she felt breathless.

"You want to kiss as much as I do," he whispered as he stepped forward and slipped his arm around her waist to draw her to him.

She stiffened, because she was crossing another line that she could never undo. And then she was lost to the moment. "Yes," she whispered, winding an arm around his neck, gazing up at him. "Damn you, Nick, for coming into my life," she added.

"I'm glad I did." His mouth came down forcefully, parting her lips as his tongue went possessively into her mouth. Heat flashed like wildfire. She tightened her arm around his neck and kissed him in return, her tongue stroking his and fanning the flames.

He clasped her close against his hard length while his other hand tangled in her hair and removed her clip. Caution vanished, consumed by passion. She thrust her hips against him, moaning softly with pleasure.

"I've wanted this since I first saw you," he whispered, and returned for more, kissing her deeply as he leaned over her and she clung to him.

His hand slid down her back. She wanted him more than ever.

The beat of her heart increased while her breathing became hoarse. Sensation blazed into a roaring inferno.

How long they kissed she didn't know. When his hand slipped lower, down over her bottom, she had to call a halt. With effort she pulled away, opening her eyes as if drugged. She desired him with an intensity that she had never known before.

"Nick, we need to stop," she whispered. Her breathing was as ragged as his. His mouth was red from kisses and her lips throbbed. She longed to step back into his embrace and continue what they'd started, but she had to end it now or she would complicate her life badly.

"I want you," he said, framing her face with his hands.

His words wrapped around her, a statement that rang with feeling. "You want something from me," she said. "This is about Michael more than you and me."

"Not this," Nick denied in a husky tone. "This has nothing to do with family, baby, or anything except a man wanting a desirable, sexy woman."

His words were a melting caress, creating havoc with her guarded intentions.

"It doesn't matter whether that's true or not. Any relationship between us is doomed. Alicia got embroiled with a Rafford and it cost her life. That thought is constantly with me."

"I've said it before—I intend to prove that I'm not Bart." Nick's arm slipped around her waist to pull her to him. "I'll never treat you the way he did Alicia. I want you in my arms in my bed and I'm determined to get what I want," he said.

"Sorry, Nick. That isn't going to happen. Your father will never give up now with Michael, but I'm not getting more deeply involved. Not with you or your family. The Raffords had their chance."

"I'm not talking about getting what my father wants. Damn it, I want you, Grace." He swooped down to kiss her again, his arm encircling her instantly and pulling her tightly against him as he kissed her passionately.

She grabbed his upper arms to stop him, but the moment his tongue thrust deeply into her mouth, her rejection transformed into need.

Passion heightened. She wound her fingers in his thick hair at the back of his head while her other hand ran across his broad shoulder. She wanted to touch and feel, kiss and be kissed.

Instead, she broke away. "Nick, stop this. We have no place in our lives for love. None whatsoever," she said, as if trying to convince herself.

His gaze traveled slowly over her features, weakening her resistance. Gently, he combed strands away from her face.

"You'll change your mind," he whispered.

"I can't," she replied, hoping she could keep him out of her life. Part of her craved the opposite. She couldn't succumb because it would be a disaster.

"Thanks again for today," he said, and turned, pausing to look at the sleeping baby. Then Nick walked out, closing the door quietly behind him.

She stepped to the window to watch him, his long, purposeful strides proclaiming his confidence.

Friday morning Nick called to arrange an afternoon appointment at her office. As they talked, he could feel the coolness in her tone of voice. Finally, she yielded and agreed to see him at her office late in the afternoon.

The moment he strolled through the door, every nerve in his body came alive. Consumed by lust, he had suffered hot, erotic fantasies that tormented him. Efforts to put her out of his mind had failed. Longing streaked in him, heating him, driving his purpose in meeting out of mind.

When their gazes locked, he could feel the sparks and she obviously experienced it, too. And just as apparent, she fought it. She sat in silence behind her desk, a convenient barrier between them.

Nick pulled a chair closer to her desk, to face her. "Thanks for seeing me," he said, sitting back to notice with satisfaction that a flush rose in her cheeks. Beneath a matching suit jacket, her vee-necked rose blouse revealed the beginning of lush curves. He longed to walk around the wooden desk and take her into his embrace. Instead, he sat quietly facing her. "How have you been?"

"Fine, Nick," she answered, and he thought she looked more gorgeous than ever. He wished she would come sit near him.

"Do you have Christmas plans?" he asked.

"I'll spend it with Michael. It'll be quiet, but fun."

"What about your aunt? Won't she be with you, too?"

"No. She leaves Monday to be with her son who is in Germany. I'll just be with Michael. So what does your father want now?" she asked.

"You're so certain my visit concerns him," Nick remarked drily.

"Doesn't it? I know you don't have designs of your own on Michael, so it has to be your father. If you just wanted to see or be with me, I don't think you'd call for an office appointment."

"You're right. My father would like to see Michael again."

As she looked away, her hands locked together on the desk. Her knuckles whitened, an obvious indication she was unhappy with his request. "You told him he could see Michael again," Nick reminded her gently.

Her gaze settled on him, glacial green that conveyed her irritation. "I know I did. That doesn't make me want to."

"Honor the request of an aging, failing grandfather."

"Stop playing on my sympathy," she flung back at him.

"I'm just stating the truth," Nick replied. While she kept her features impassive, he could see the battle raging inside her.

"Very well," she said, relenting. "I know I told him he could see Michael."

"Thank you, Grace," Nick said. "Christmas is next weekend. Come visit Christmas Eve. Have dinner with us and stay over Christmas morning. Then you can go home and have your Christmas with Michael. That way, I'll enjoy Christmas."

"I think that's way more visiting than I intended when I told your father we would see him again."

"Look, you don't have plans. You've already told me that. This may be Dad's last Christmas. Michael's presence would give him so much joy. Your presence will give *me* pleasure," Nick added, wanting her to agree. He wasn't looking forward to Christmas Eve and morning with his dad, something they never used to do, yet something he felt duty-bound to do now.

"Nick, I don't care to spend my Christmas with your dad."

Nick stood and walked around the desk, pulling her chair

out and grasping her waist to draw her to her feet. Frowning, she opened her mouth, he guessed, to protest. He took advantage and leaned down, covering her mouth with his.

Momentarily, she was stiff in his arms and then she yielded, wrapping an arm around his neck. His body heated with white-hot desire as he leaned over her and kissed her hungrily, pouring out the lust he'd felt in her absence. He savored the kiss, the softness of her mouth, the sensual feel of her tongue. Her body was curvaceous, lush and warm against him. He tangled his hand in her hair, which had been pinned on her head. He didn't care. He intended to kiss away her remoteness and elicit a response and an acceptance from her.

He could feel her heart thumping against his, hear her soft moans that raced through him like lightning. He wanted to lay her down on her desk and make love to her now, but that was impossible.

Instead, he tore his mouth away to look at her as she gasped. Her eyes slowly opened. "Spend Christmas with me," he demanded. "You'll be alone otherwise. I want you there with me. Will you?"

"Yes," she whispered, looking dazed. Fire now replaced the frost in her green eyes. Her lips were red, full, an enticing temptation. He dipped his head again to kiss her, stopping any words.

She arched against him, holding him tightly while her fingers tangled in his hair. He throbbed with need and was hard, ready. They had to go slowly, because they were racing headlong into a depth that would complicate and heighten the friction between them.

"Stop, Nick. We're in my office," she gasped. She gulped air and her protest was weak, but he stepped away.

She smoothed her hair that had too many strands pulled loose to put back in place. As he watched, she took it down and shook her head. He reached out, winding his fingers in her silky, thick hair.

"Your hair is beautiful, Grace," he whispered. He leaned forward to brush a kiss on her throat. "I want to bury my hands in it."

"Nick, my assistant could come in."

"She won't. I asked her to see to it that you're not disturbed," he whispered, trailing kisses to her nape and hearing her intake of breath. He placed his hand against her throat and could feel her racing pulse, which gave him a stab of satisfaction.

He straightened, dropping his hands to his sides. "You agreed to Christmas Eve with me and Christmas morning."

"I know," she whispered, her reluctance obvious.

"I promise to see to it you have a good time."

"You can't possibly promise that," she said without conviction in her voice. He couldn't keep from smiling at her.

"It'll be a Christmas to remember forever," he said.

"Watch what you promise," she warned, the frost returning to her gaze. "Now you go back and sit where you were unless you're leaving."

He gripped her hand. "Come here." Circling the desk, he held a chair facing his. "Sit here and stop keeping the damned desk between us. I want to talk to you before I go."

"Have you always spent Christmas Eve and morning with your father?" she asked as she sat, her question surprising him.

Pulling his chair closer to hers, Nick shook his head. "No. There were a lot of holidays when he would go off to Europe with my current stepmother. I stayed with a friend," he answered without thinking about his reply. His thoughts were on Grace because her disheveled appearance made him think of hot sex. Her hair tumbled around her face, cascading across her shoulders, a thick, wild mane that was a sensual invitation.

Her lips were just-been-kissed red. Desire glowed in the depths of her gaze, making it difficult to think about their conversation when what he wanted to do was draw her back into his embrace and continue kissing her.

"You never had to stay at the boarding school?"

"No. When I was young, I think Dad arranged with a friend's family to get me invited, probably showering them with presents for taking me in. When I was older, I had friends who would invite me because they knew I wasn't going home."

"That's dreadful, Nick," she said, staring at him as if he had sprouted two heads. "I'm amazed you spend your Christmases with him now if he abandoned you that much on holidays in your childhood."

Nick shrugged. "I didn't until these last two years when his health failed. And now he's lost Bart. I guess I love the old man and I feel sorry for him. He's having a tough time. I don't have anything to gain by going off and leaving him alone for Christmas. That would be selfish on my part. What he did is his own worry. What I do is mine."

"That's good of you," she said in a strange voice, studying him intently. He wondered whether he had won her over slightly with his reply and hoped that was the reason behind the sharp stare.

"Christmas Eve with us will be better than staying alone with a baby who'll sleep a good deal of the time. Also, Dad would like to have a professional photographer out to get some Christmas photos with Michael."

She had to laugh. "Nick, a *professional* photographer? As I told your dad, it's fine with me—as long as I get a picture, too. That will be wonderful and something I could never afford."

"See?" he said. "Dad's money can do things you like," he reminded her lightly and she wrinkled her nose at him. "How about I pick you up around five o'clock on Christmas Eve?"

"Make it half past five, please. I have a lot of party-planning to do, and I won't have Clara to help with Michael."

"Half past five it is. Excellent," he said, wishing the weekend started tonight and he could be with Grace. "I'm looking forward to this holiday, something I definitely was not doing until a minute ago."

The pink deepened in her cheeks. "Don't be ridiculous," she replied lightly.

"Before I go, there's one more thing. It's important and before you give me an answer, take a few days to think about it. I expect you to refuse my request, but give it consideration." The minute the words were spoken, she stiffened and he could feel an invisible barrier rising between them. Her frostiness returned, along with a wary look in her eyes.

"What's that, Nick? What else do you want of me?"

"My dad would like Michael to legally have the Rafford name," Nick stated.

She locked her fingers together in her lap. "He doesn't waste time. No. That would basically give Michael to your family."

"No, it won't. Just a legal last-name change. The name does not put him in my family and Dad knows that. Think about this request before you decide. I can see the refusal in your expression. Consider what I'm telling you. Dad will set up a trust for Michael. Right now, he will open an account that you can use for him. This would help you out with the baby and pay for his college. No giant fortune, just a reasonable sum to see that he's educated."

"Stop, Nick," she ordered, looking into his dark eyes. "I don't want Rafford money. I don't really need it. I'm not changing the baby's name from Vaughan, Alicia's name. You're on a futile mission and wasting your breath. Neither threats nor bribes will win me over."

"I'm not going to threaten you with anything," he said, smiling at her and causing her slight frown to vanish. "Look, why deny Michael the benefit of this? Michael is a Rafford—why not let him have the name?"

"The Vaughan name is a tie to his mother."

"Do you really want to take this away from Michael?"

"I don't think I'm taking anything from him," she argued. "I'll take care of Michael, send him to college, and I don't need your father's money."

"My father is a generous man," Nick said quietly, wondering if she had any concept of the fortune she was refusing. It was an effort to hold on to his patience. Who turned down money and a deal like the one his dad was offering? "We're not talking small change here," he couldn't resist tossing out.

"It doesn't matter," she said. "I won't do this. He wants Michael to be a Rafford. Next thing, he would want Michael to stay with him. He can hire nannies easily. Then he'd want to keep Michael and move me into his mansion, unless he tries to just get rid of me."

"You're jumping to conclusions."

"No, I'm not," she stated. "Your dad is after my baby. End of discussion, Nick. We won't argue through Christmas Eve over this issue, will we?"

"No," he said, wondering if he could keep his word on that one. "I'll tell Dad your answer. He'll have to abandon the idea for now."

"For now and forever." She stood and he came to his feet. He had achieved an important part of his quest. He would get to spend Christmas Eve and morning with her. The prospect pleased him and he intended to use the time to win her friendship. In the meantime, he'd have to deal with his father's disappointment. Not that his father would relent in his pursuit of the name change.

Nick postponed telling his dad until the next day. His father's anger worried Nick because it couldn't be good for his heart. He had to think of some way to convince Grace to agree.

Michael Rafford. How simple it would be, yet Grace had been adamant. Nick raked his fingers through his hair, mulling over ideas, finally beginning to settle on one that he had originally rejected instantly.

Three nights later in the club dining room with one of his close friends, Nick mentioned his plan. Jake Benton's jaw dropped and he stared at Nick.

"I think your brain has stopped functioning."

"I've thought about it. A marriage of convenience—I legally adopt my nephew. We end the sham marriage after Dad's gone. The marriage puts a crimp in my life for only a little while."

"Suppose your dad recovers fully and is here another twenty years? You'd be married to a woman you don't love and vice versa, raising your brother's child. The last wouldn't be bad, but the other terrible. Don't do it."

"We could divorce. She'd get the benefits of the Rafford money because she would be part of the family."

"You'd have to share the fortune."

Nick shrugged. "Not really. I'll be Dad's heir because I'll agree to make Michael and Grace my beneficiaries. She's not a gold digger or she would have gone after Dad's money when she had the chance. If something happens to Dad and then to me—I don't have heirs anyway."

Jake tilted his head, his deep blue-eyed gaze intent. "I guess you have a point there. Michael is Bart's child, so that would be good. You'll make your dad happy."

"Yes. If I can talk Grace into this."

"She'd be crazy to turn you down."

"She's independent as hell and fighting to keep us from latching on to Michael. She's scared of losing him."

"She's his mother and he's actually been her baby from the start from what you've told me," Jake said. "I guess I can see how you came up with the idea, but a loveless marriage is scary as hell. Marriage is scary as hell. Look at our dads and their failed marriages and the misery it gave everyone."

"It'll be a cut-and-dried business deal," Nick said, thinking about Grace's kisses. "Sort of."

"Not exactly cut-and-dried," Jake replied in a sarcastic tone. "I saw her. Sparks were flying between the two of you when you didn't know each other. There won't be anything cut-and-dried about a marriage to her. She's hot," Jake said. "You'll sink like you're in a tar pit."

Nick grinned as he shook his head. "I don't think you can compare her to a tar pit, and you're right about hot. No, I guess it might turn out to be exciting."

"Watch out, Nick. You're going to complicate your life terribly. You'll also lose a million dollars in that bet we made."

"I can stand the million. I don't want to lose my dad's fortune."

"I don't blame you. No matter how old they get, our dads can't stop trying to manipulate everyone around them. That's one reason you and Tony and I got to be close friends—shoved together first by our dads and then sticking together because we all had the same kind of dad—driven, controlling."

"If you stop and think about it, we're probably somewhat that way ourselves now."

"I hope to hell not," Jake said, with a dark look at Nick. "Are you telling Tony this harebrained scheme of yours?"

"If I see him, I will."

"Well, I don't think any of us, you included, can say a marriage of convenience would work. Even to a woman like you have in mind. We three know firsthand the likelihood of a successful marriage. At least in the circles we've moved in. I suppose if you go into it with low expectations, you won't be disappointed."

"I have high expectations of getting back in Dad's will. That's my prime goal. Grace and I should be able to develop a workable arrangement and she won't be hanging on me, falling in love with me."

"Suppose you fall in love—I don't need to ask that one. You won't. I know you as well as I know myself. No such thing will happen. We were disillusioned long ago."

"If you're through eating, we might as well head to the poker game. Tony may be there by now," Nick said, drinking the last of his water and standing. As the two men left the luxurious club dining room, Nick fell into step beside Jake in the hallway.

"By the way, are you going to the private horse sale at the Jenkins ranch next month?" Nick asked.

"I wouldn't miss it. Tad Jenkins has the best horses around."

"I agree. We'll be bidding against each other," Nick said, and Jake grinned.

"I won't bid if you start first and you don't if I start first—how's that?" Jake suggested.

"Sounds okay. Every horse he sells will be prime horseflesh."

"You'll miss it if you're on a honeymoon."

Nick shook his head. "Nothing will interfere with my attendance at that sale. I can work a wedding around it."

"Does the little lady ride?"

"I have no idea, nor do I care. I have other plans for my time spent with her," Nick said and Jake laughed.

"Good luck with your crazy scheme. I hope you know what you're doing. I'm one step closer to winning our bet."

"I know what I'm doing. Now if I can just convince Grace," Nick said, deciding Christmas Eve would be the time to propose.

Six

Monday before Christmas, Grace kissed her aunt goodbye. Clara would not be back to Dallas until after the first of the year.

"Have a wonderful time with your son," Grace said, hugging Clara. "Glenda will be here part of the time to help with Michael, so you enjoy yourself."

"I will, but I'll miss Michael. You take care," Clara said solemnly. "I'll worry about you Christmas Eve. I know Eli Rafford wants Michael and will keep after you until he gets what he wants."

"Stop worrying. I won't let that happen. An immediate worry is what do I give them for gifts. Both men have everything they want," she said, having spent the past week wondering about what to give Nick.

"You'll think of something. You've already given Eli Rafford the best gift possible in taking Michael for Christmas.

Take care of yourself and Michael," Clara said again. "And I want one of those copies of the Christmas photographs."

Grace gave her aunt another hug and watched her hurry to her car. She turned away, thinking about what to give the Rafford men—impossible task.

That night and the days and nights to follow, Grace was busy catering Christmas parties until Christmas Eve arrived. The booked parties were over until the day after Christmas when they started up again.

It took the afternoon to get ready to go to Eli Rafford's for the night. As she packed, the butterflies in her stomach grew worse. She dreaded dealing with Michael's grandfather while excitement mounted over being with Nick again.

She picked up Michael, smoothing his thick black hair. He was dressed in a navy jumper and a white sweater. She kissed his cheek. "You look adorable," she told him, smiling at him as he cooed and babbled. "Now please don't spit up on my sweater," she said to him, turning to look at both of them in an oval mirror. Her hair was clipped behind her head and she wore a red sweater and red wool skirt—maybe a poor choice with a baby. She glanced down at him. "Remember, no formula on this sweater, please. This is your first Christmas, sweetie."

She looked around her tiny living room, at the Christmas tree placed on a table to keep it away from Michael, who crawled well now. She had a few presents under the tree for him, but he was too little to open his gifts. She could imagine the toys that awaited him from his grandfather.

The doorbell rang and she hurried to face Nick, whose intent gaze knotted her insides as always.

"Merry Christmas," he said, smiling at her while she motioned for him to come inside. He stepped in, filling the narrow hallway and moving into the living area. "Ah, you're all ready for Christmas," he said, walking to her tree. In a black topcoat over his suit, he dominated her small living room, which seemed to shrink in size when he entered.

"Our tree isn't fancy, but he's too little to know what's happening. He's beginning to crawl, so I had to keep it out of his reach," she said, while putting on Michael's coat and then buckling him into his carrier.

"Good idea. Dad had a child's fence put around ours. We have a nanny for the evening to help you with Michael, so you can eat in peace and quiet. If it's all right with you, we'll let her give him a bottle if he wants one while we eat."

"Thank you. That's fine," she said. She would be present to make certain Michael was taken care of, yet it would give her a chance to enjoy eating without interruptions. If Michael was awake, she rarely got through a meal without being disturbed.

"I didn't think you'd object, since we'll all be right there. She came with high recommendations," he said, smiling. He turned to her and her heart missed a beat.

"I'm sure she did," she said. "It will be a nice change."

Nick walked up to place his hands on her shoulders. "I've missed seeing you."

"Nick, there's not much point in us seeing each other."

"I don't know about that. We have Michael between us. I have a feeling we're in each other's lives for a long time to come." Her heart drummed as she looked into his warm dark eyes. "You look beautiful, Grace," he said in a husky voice.

"Thank you." She gazed up at him, thinking he looked energetic, sexy, appealing.

In turn, he looked amused as he studied her. "I'd rather stay right here with you," Nick said in a deep voice. "My dad is waiting, though. He's been counting the minutes until it was time to get you. Otherwise, we wouldn't rush back."

"But since he is waiting, we should go. Besides, Michael

will eventually stop sitting quietly and amusing himself in his carrier."

"Do you have an overnight bag packed?" Nick asked, picking up the carrier with Michael and glancing around.

She slipped into her long black coat. "Yes, a bag for each of us and a small box of toys and things for Michael."

Nick took the bags from her hands, shouldered them, picked up Michael and opened the door. Carrying the box of toys, she turned off the lights, locked up and left with him.

"Christmas Eve," she said.

"We'll always remember spending it together," Nick reminded her. "Have you been busy constantly?"

"Yes. The past hour has been my quietest for the entire week."

"I can imagine. I could have rescued you from that, whisked you away until tonight. Next time, let me know."

"Thanks, but I had work to do. We've had parties booked day and night, so I couldn't have escaped had I wanted to."

"Get ready for a party yourself. Small party, that is. Dad is as excited as a kid about tonight."

"It's a grand holiday," she said.

"This is definitely the best part," Nick said.

She remained in the grip of excitement as they drove through the estate grounds once again. A cold front and a dense fog were settling in and it was cozy in Nick's car. Michael cooed in the back as they wound up the driveway. The minute they stepped inside, she drew a deep breath, reminded again of the Raffords' wealth and power.

The mansion had been turned into a winter wonderland. Trees with myriad lights sparkled at spaced intervals along the great hallway.

"Nick," she said, halting to stare at the enormous tree standing between the two curving staircases. It had to be at least twenty feet tall and decorated with hundreds of twinkling ornaments. "This is fit for royalty."

"My father probably thinks he *is* royalty," Nick remarked drily. "It's just a big tree."

"Maybe to you, because you've grown up with trees like it. To me, it's magical, amazing. How I wish Michael knew what he was seeing. It's magnificent."

"That's not the family tree. It's in the great room and that's where we'll spend the evening."

Garlands of greenery and red ribbons draped the banisters of the winding staircases. "Michael, look," she said to the baby in his carrier, "Isn't it beautiful? Nick, this is enchanting. I'm sorry he's too little to know what's here."

"He will next year," Nick said, and she gave him a startled glance. She hadn't thought in the long term about Eli and Nick remaining in her life. The thought of them becoming permanent in her life had just become more real.

"I brought presents in that bag you're carrying," she said.

"You didn't need to. Michael would have been enough of a gift."

She walked beside Nick, overwhelmed again by her surroundings, wondering why she had ever thought for a second that she wouldn't be diminished, made to feel insignificant the minute she entered the mansion again.

They passed through the wide double doors to the great room, where Nick told her most receptions and formal parties were held. Another huge tree, this one white, was festooned with ribbons and more sparkling ornaments and bows. She stopped in front of it in awe. "What fantastic Christmases you must have had," she said, momentarily forgetting what he had told her about his childhood holidays.

"Some years I wasn't here," he reminded her, and she turned to stare at him.

"I'm sorry, Nick," she said. "Now I think it was best that

Bart didn't marry Alicia, not that he ever had any intention of doing so. Michael would have grown up in the same manner."

"Good evening," came a voice behind them and she turned to see Eli Rafford enter the room. He crossed over to shake her hand and then looked down at Michael as Nick removed the baby from his carrier.

"Ah, he's a fine-looking boy. Thank you so much for coming. I've looked forward to this since you accepted my invitation. I think he's grown in the past few days."

She smiled as Nick took her coat to hand it to a staff member who had materialized quietly. Grace took Michael from Nick, watching while Nick put her presents around the foot of the huge tree along with a mound of gifts already under the tree. She looked at the luxurious Christmas trimmings and thought about her own meager decorations and single, small tree and wondered how Michael would feel about his two families. She was certain the Raffords were in her and Michael's life to stay. Unless Eli tried to get rid of her.

She glanced up at Nick, who turned to look into her eyes with a questioning expression.

"I'll take Michael's things to the nursery where Vanessa, the nanny, is," Nick said, picking up a bag and leaving.

"Oh, my word!" For the first time she noticed stockings hung on the mammoth fireplace, one for each of them, including one with her name and one with Michael's.

"We have stockings."

"Of course we do," Eli said, chuckling. "It's Christmas. They are hung for Santa. Now, let me hold my precious grandchild," he added. "Come sit near us, Grace, and tell me more about Michael."

After placing Michael in Eli's arms, she sat close in a wing chair. As frail as Eli appeared when he was standing, his arms looked strong and his hands large, and he seemed to have a firm grip on Michael, who was happily playing with a teething ring.

Nick returned to sit near them, facing her. As she talked, she was aware of Nick listening, watching her with a faint smile on his face. Once she caught him studying her legs and when he glanced up and their eyes met, his were hot, filled with so much desire that her heart skipped.

"The photographer should be here right away. Thank you for consenting to pictures."

"It'll be great to have Christmas pictures of Michael," she responded.

It was only minutes later the photographer was announced and for the next hour, pictures were taken and then the photographer packed his equipment and was gone.

"Michael is a happy baby," Eli observed. "What a marvel he is. A special baby. Your sharing him with us this Christmas is the greatest possible Christmas gift."

"It's good for the two of you to know each other," she said. Under different circumstances, she would have been delighted to find the grandfather and uncle in Michael's life. As it was, her fear of Eli had been pushed aside slightly for this evening.

When Michael became wiggly, she spread a small blanket on the floor and put some of his toys on it, setting him down. He sat happily playing before beginning to crawl around. She scooped him up. "He's getting around better every day. He likes to explore."

"Let's go meet the nanny and I'll show you Dad's new nursery. Excuse us, Dad. We'll be back shortly."

As they entered the hall, Nick reached out to take Michael from her. "I'll carry him. You've probably carried him for hours."

"Actually, yes I have. I don't mind yet because he's not too heavy."

"Sometime I'll give you the grand tour of this house."

She laughed. "I hope I don't get lost tonight. And Michael will be staying in my room, right?"

"Unless you want a different arrangement. If you don't want him in the same room, he can stay in the nursery with Vanessa, because she's staying the night."

"I'd rather have him with me when I go to bed. He sleeps through the night, but I wouldn't want him to wake in a strange place with someone he barely knows."

"I figured that. Vanessa will put him to bed in the room where you'll sleep and she'll sit in there with him until you turn in. Then she'll stay in her own room. We have a third floor filled with staff who live here. As you could see driving up, there's as much room as a hotel."

"A very large hotel," she said. "Michael may not be happy going home with me someday when he grows accustomed to what he has here."

Nick gave her an inscrutable look and she wondered what was on his mind. "Why the look?" she asked.

"Just thinking about what you said. You're his mother and you love him. He'll always be happy going with you. Here we are," Nick said, taking her arm while he carried Michael with his other arm. They entered a large, enchanting nursery that reminded her again of the Raffords' wealth. The room held a double bed, a baby crib, dressers, tables, a rocking chair, two other chairs, and was decorated with nursery rhyme decor. A bin contained toys. A tall blond woman stood when they entered.

"Grace, this is Vanessa Otis. Vanessa, meet Grace Wayland, and this is Michael."

"He's adorable," Vanessa said, taking the baby from Nick. "Hi, Michael," she said to him before smiling at Grace. "When did he last eat?"

"He'll probably be hungry soon because it's been long

enough since the last bottle. I brought formula, bottles, baby food, and he takes some finger food. Everything is in his bag."

"I have Michael's bag with his things and I can fix the bottles. I have six younger siblings, so I'm accustomed to babies," she said, smiling at Grace, and Nick waited while Grace gave instructions about Michael's bottle.

When they left, Nick walked beside her. "Are you going to worry about him?"

"No. Vanessa seemed competent, and I imagine she has plenty of credentials, in addition to her own siblings, and has been thoroughly checked out."

"You're right. She has some great recommendations, but I wanted to be sure you were comfortable."

"Actually, I imagine I'll enjoy dinner more. When I'm home, I never sit through a meal without interruptions."

He smiled. "Yet you love taking care of him."

"Of course. I love him. He's precious and I can't wait to get home to him every day. So what's our schedule here, Nick? Are presents opened tonight or tomorrow?"

"Tomorrow morning. We'll have the Christmas meal tonight and Dad will go to bed early. This has been great for him, Grace. He's trying to make it nice for you because he appreciates having Michael more than you can guess."

"It's easy to do this now while Michael is a baby," she said, wondering what the future held. Her problems had diminished with Nick's presence because she was so aware of him. He was close, tempting. She would be alone with him later and the prospect was exciting.

When they joined Eli again, Megan was with him. Dinner was served in a large dining room that could have easily accommodated twenty at the table. It was a lavish spread and the food was delicious, but it was difficult to eat with

Nick seated across from her, his smoldering dark eyes on her, holding promises of hot kisses later.

After dinner, Vanessa brought Michael in his pajamas to play in the great room. At his bedtime, she scooped him up, promising to rock him to sleep, and Grace kissed him and let Vanessa carry him to bed. Half an hour later, Eli apologized, saying he had to turn in for the night. Megan held his arm as they left the room.

Nick tossed another log on the fire, crossed the room to close the wide double doors and came back. "Let me show you something," he said.

She stood to go with him and they headed toward the doors he had just closed. He stopped in front of them, but didn't reach to open them and she gave him a puzzled look.

"You haven't noticed," he said, glancing up.

She looked up to see the mistletoe tied with a bright red velvet bow hanging above her head.

He shook his head. "I've been waiting since the last time we were together. We're under the mistletoe." His arm circled her waist and he leaned forward to kiss her, pulling her tightly into his embrace.

"Since when do you need mistletoe?" she whispered, before their lips touched. She slipped her arms around him and stood on tiptoe while her heartbeat galloped.

Pressing against his hard body, she felt his erection thrust against her. She ached for him, wanting him, knowing each time they were together she was becoming more involved with him. This holiday was going to bind her closer than ever. While he kissed her, nothing else really mattered. His kisses fanned desire to greater heights. She needed more, wanted his hands and his mouth on her. All evening the looks he had given her, the slight contacts had increased her longing until she felt she would burst.

"Nick," she whispered, and crushed her mouth to his for

more kisses, moaning as her hips plunged against him. He held her tightly with one arm, his other hand trailing down her back languidly, a sensual caress. His hand slipped over her bottom, following her curves and then slid around her waist.

Slipping beneath her red sweater, his large, warm hands pushed away wispy lace and cupped her breasts. She moaned with pleasure as her tongue thrust deeply over his.

She heard his deep-throated groan while his thumbs circled each taut bud. Waves of pleasure washed over her. Eagerly she ran her hands over his powerful shoulders, removing his jacket, to unbutton his shirt. His sculpted chest was rock hard with a thick mat of black curls. She tangled her fingers in black, wiry chest hair, relishing touching him.

He leaned over her, his passionate kisses going deep, heightening her response. Within minutes they had to stop or they'd be beyond stopping. She tore her mouth from his while caressing his chest, her signals as mixed as her feelings.

"Nick, we have to stop," she whispered.

"Why?" he asked, raising his head. He continued to caress her breasts while his gaze slowly devoured her. "You're beautiful," he whispered, his thumbs rubbing each nipple.

Fighting her own desire, she clutched his hands. "No more," she whispered, unable to find a strong voice.

"Why? We're alone. No one will disturb us," Nick said.

"I didn't come here tonight to sleep with you. I'm not ready for intimacy. I'm not making love at your father's house," she said. "Lust isn't the point of this visit."

"It's what we both want," Nick said bluntly.

She stepped back, slipping her bra into place as he watched her. While she straightened her clothes, her heart raced. Nick stood inches away, his hair tangled from her fingers. His shirt was open and his muscled chest captured her attention. His trousers indicated his arousal. He wanted her and he looked seductive, appealing.

Her heart hammered loudly. With an effort to break his spell she intended to stick with what she had told him.

"You and I shouldn't make love. Not tonight. Most likely not ever. I don't care how great the kisses are," she whispered. "We've got Michael, different views and opposing goals between us. I'm not succumbing to desire, because it will only complicate everything between us a thousand times over. We're not in love. We're not in agreement. Your family, you because of your dad, wants Michael. I don't want you to have him. It's that simple, and seduction would be an emotional disaster."

"It doesn't have to be," Nick stated, studying her.

"This has been a nice evening, but we should each go our separate way now."

"If that's what you want, Grace," he replied. As he buttoned his shirt, she struggled to get a grip on her emotions. Resisting the urge to walk right back into his arms and toss aside her declarations, she shook her head, smoothing her hair away from her face.

"C'mon, I'll give you a partial tour and show you where you'll sleep. You and I are in the east wing, where the nursery is." He led her down a large hall.

"How did you ever get used to this?" she asked.

"I grew up in it. Parts were off-limits for play for years. When I outgrew that restriction, I went everywhere. This was my home and I got used to it just like you do your home."

He directed her through an open door and switched on a light. She stood in an elegant suite with decor in shades of brown and tan.

"Here's where I am, should you want to come talk," Nick said. Grace gave him a sharp look to see amusement in his eyes.

"And my room?"

They returned to the hall and entered another suite. The pink and white looked done by a decorator, just as his had, with elegant white furniture and bright pink accessories. Pink and green Christmas decorations adorned the sitting room, which had a decorated white tree standing in a corner. Beyond the sitting room she could see a bedroom. When she stepped to the door, she saw a baby crib on one side of the room. Vanessa came forward with a book in her hand.

"Michael is sleeping. He hasn't stirred since I put him in his bed."

"Thank you so much," Grace said.

"He's a sweet, happy baby. I'll go to bed now," Vanessa said as she headed for the door.

"Thanks, Vanessa," Nick said. "We'll see you in the morning." Nick and Grace strolled to the sitting room where Nick stepped ahead to hold the door for Vanessa. When they were alone, he walked back to Grace.

"I can watch him tomorrow morning."

"Dad will want him with us for the opening of the presents. He's been talking about this for a week and you know he has toys for Michael."

"I can imagine," she said.

Nick reached beyond her and pulled a sprig of mistletoe off the Christmas tree to dangle the sprig above her head. "One kiss beneath the mistletoe," he said. Without waiting for her answer, he kissed her, holding her close.

She remained immobile for a moment, but then wrapped her arms around him, her exasperation vanishing instantly as desire fanned to life again.

She moaned and poured herself into their kiss, returning his passion, her senses coming to life as longing assailed her stronger than ever.

She had no idea how long they kissed, but she finally ended it. "Nick, nothing has changed since we kissed earlier."

"I'll leave now, but sometime you'll want me to stay. You'll let me make love to you because you want me just as much as I want you. We don't have a battle between us. Because of my dad, you're conjuring up demons. But you and I don't have a real struggle going. Far from it," Nick said, stroking a strand of hair away from her face.

"Nick, you should go," she whispered, his words as seductive as his caresses and his kisses.

He brushed another kiss lightly on her lips, tossed the sprig of mistletoe onto a table and turned, walking to the door where he paused. "If you want to talk, I'm right there. Knock on the wall and I'll come so you don't have to leave Michael."

"Forget any knocking on the wall," she said in amusement. He grinned and left, closing the door behind him.

Looking around the suite, she noticed the mistletoe and picked up the sprig. With a glance at the white tree and its pink decorations, she noticed there weren't any other sprigs of mistletoe. Had Nick put that sprig on the tree?

She peeked at Michael, who was sleeping on his knees facedown on the Co-Sleeper attached to the bed. He wore footed pajamas and had his stuffed bunny clutched in his hand. Filled with love, Grace touched his head. She couldn't keep his grandfather from seeing him or being with him. She wished she could just trust that Eli didn't intend to try to take Michael from her.

When she slid into bed, she guessed Nick would fill her dreams as he had every night for a week.

Christmas morning she showered and was dressed in a green sweater and slacks before Michael stirred. "Merry Christmas, love," she said as she picked him up and nuzzled him. He smelled of baby powder and he clutched her shoulder while she carried him.

When she had Michael dressed in his red Santa suit, she left her suite. Nick's door stood open and he appeared. "Merry Christmas," he said, smiling at her.

Casually dressed in a navy sweater and chinos, he looked dangerous, sexy, appealing.

"Merry Christmas, Nick," she said as he walked up to her to kiss her lightly.

"Merry Christmas to you," she said.

"Good morning, Michael," Nick said, and the baby smiled at him.

"Look at you, getting a smile first thing. He barely knows you."

"He knows I'm his uncle," Nick said. "And he's glad to see me, just as I am glad to see you both. Sleep well?"

"Of course," she answered.

"Let's do Christmas. Dad can't wait to give Michael a present. I don't think he ever got excited over either Bart or me on Christmas morning."

"He might have when you were very young," she said.

"We were in his way when he was young. Now, he's changed. His illness has turned him into a different man. Many of those driving goals he had are gone and the people around him get his full attention."

"Michael is probably hungry. He's a very good baby, but I don't want to keep him waiting."

In the kitchen Vanessa waited. As soon as she saw them, she came to take Michael from Grace. "How adorable he is," she said, smiling at Michael. "Michael is happy all the time. I'll feed him and you can eat your breakfast. Mr. Rafford and Megan are in the great room. They've already eaten and have coffee waiting for you in there."

Grace handed over Michael and joined Nick at the table. The cook brought plates of eggs and toast. After they finished, they joined Eli and Megan by the Christmas tree. Little toys filled Michael's stocking and his toys sat at the foot of the tree.

"Santa has been here," Eli said with twinkling eyes. His color was better and he looked stronger than when Grace had met him, causing her to wonder how big an influence Michael was in his life.

Grace left to get her cameras. When she returned, she saw that Eli also had a camcorder and a camera ready, and she laughed. "I think this baby is going to be a celebrity this morning and he'll have no idea what's going on. It'll be a thoroughly documented first Christmas."

Nick smiled. "Dad wants every minute caught. We'll start with Michael though I know he can't open anything."

"No, he would promptly put the wrappings in his mouth." As Vanessa handed her the baby, Grace said, "I'll put him on the floor and let's see if he gets one of his toys first." She set Michael down and picked up her own camcorder. He promptly crawled to a transparent ball filled with plastic butterflies and glittering spheres that played tunes when he rolled it around.

In minutes they were immersed in gifts and Nick handed her a box with a lovely blue ribbon that she intended to take home and keep. It was from Nick and as she opened it, she guessed he had one of the women who worked for him do his shopping.

It was a silver frame that would be perfect for Michael's picture and she looked up, smiling at Nick. "You know I love this. It's beautiful and perfect."

"Great," he replied, his eyes filled with a special look that thrilled her and made her forget they were in a room with others.

"Now I'll open yours," he said, taking a present and sitting near her as he tore it open. Startled, he looked up at her. "Where did you get these?" he asked, surprise in his voice.

He lifted out two framed pictures of the last rodeo he'd been in as he rode a bucking horse.

"I'd read about you in rodeos in a Texas magazine, so I called around and finally found the pictures. I hope you don't already have them."

"No," he said, smiling. "I don't, and I'm happy you tracked them down. Thank you," he said, and she had another tingle because his tone made the statement personal, carrying silent meaning. He might as well have been blatantly flirting for the effect he was causing. She watched as he walked to the tree and picked up one of her presents for Eli.

The moment Eli opened the box and removed a scrapbook filled with photos of Michael, he smiled at her. "Grace, what a treasure! You couldn't have possibly given me anything that would please me more. I'm so grateful," he said, flipping through the pages." He looked at her and his eyes filled with tears. "Thank you. This means more than you know," he said, his voice cracking.

"I'm glad," she replied, surprised by his reaction, which was far deeper than she had expected. She could feel the barriers around her heart develop cracks, a dangerous reaction.

It took most of the morning to get through the presents and to watch and film Michael, plus getting snapshots of him with each of them.

Lunch was long and leisurely, and filled with stories from Eli of other generations of Raffords, and then they spent another hour playing with Michael before he fell asleep. While Michael slept they went to the lavish entertainment room to watch a Christmas movie, which was timed perfectly with Michael's nap that ended as the movie finished.

It was almost five in the afternoon before Grace told Nick she should go home. She thought Eli was beginning to droop. Goodbyes took another twenty minutes. Finally she was in the car with Nick. The day had become overcast, a fog settling in, bringing darkness early.

"You made my dad a very happy man today. You can't imagine how much this meant to him."

"That's good," she said, wondering how Nick truly felt about his nephew. Michael had to have cut into Nick's life and caused upheaval in trying to please his dad's wishes. She glanced back at the sleeping baby. "I think Michael is worn to a frazzle. His brief nap this afternoon helped, but he may sleep through the night now, since he ate just before we left your dad's."

"I imagine Dad is worn to a frazzle, too. He usually has catnaps and he missed them. All in all, the visit was fantastic."

"You sound surprised."

"I'll have to admit, I am. I knew it would be good to be with you, but we had a house filled with people—Dad, Vanessa, Megan and the rest of the staff constantly present. I wanted to be alone with you, but today was enjoyable and I'll admit, I'm surprised by my feelings for my nephew. I've never been around kids, never thought about them. I haven't particularly cared to get to know any if I'm briefly around them. Michael is cute and he can certainly win you over, which is funny, because he can't converse and he drools."

She laughed. "So you like him after all. He's adorable and who could resist him?" she said, her smile vanishing as she wondered if today had simply reinforced Eli's determination to get Michael into the Rafford family and hereafter it would be easier to enlist Nick's help.

"Don't start worrying," Nick said quietly.

"I hate that. You easily guess my thoughts while I never have the remotest idea what's on your mind."

"You should be able to guess exactly what's on my mind,"

he said, his suggestive tone carrying a sexy innuendo that made her forget the past day, problems and others.

"I want to be alone with you," Nick said, his tone stirring more shivers. "We've spent Christmas without a single kiss."

"We kissed early this morning when I first saw you."

"That one hardly counts," he said.

She didn't want to tell him that even the slight brush of his lips on hers this morning had stirred a heated response. Nick's looks, his presence, his kisses, always brought a reaction. He had to know the effect he had on women.

At her apartment Michael stirred and Nick waited while she fed Michael, changed him and put him to bed.

"He's out for the night this time, I'm sure," she said. "We'll have our little Christmas tomorrow morning," she said, coming back into her living room, which now seemed smaller than ever. Lights glowed on her tree and she wondered if she looked poor to Nick. He would never understand her refusal of his father's monetary offer.

Nick crossed the room to her. "Merry Christmas," he said, taking her into his arms. His gaze lowered to her mouth and she forgot everything else. His tongue parted her lips, thrust deeply into her mouth to stroke her tongue.

Melting, she clung to him, kissing him hotly in return, wanting to rattle him as much as he had her. He had sent her life into an upheaval with his passionate kisses. They were headed for a blowup because of their struggle over Michael. She was entangled with Nick now and there was no turning back on that. All she could do was fight to keep her baby, but she was beyond the point of resisting Nick. Each time they were together he became more important and had a stronger effect on her. When he wasn't present, he was in her thoughts far too much of the time.

Continuing to kiss her, Nick picked her up to carry her to the sofa where he sat down with her on his lap. She could feel his arousal pressed against her, hard and ready.

He cradled her against his shoulder while his hand stroked her hip and slid to her waist. His other hand wrapped around her, his fingers slipping beneath her sweater to take away her bra and caress her breast.

While moaning with relish, she ran her fingers through his thick, short hair, caressing his nape. She wasn't aware of his fingers unfastening her slacks until he shoved them away and slid his hand across her bare belly, his fingers moving lower, touching her between her thighs intimately.

She tried to twist away to protest, but he continued kissing her. She caught his hand to inch him away and he merely drifted to caress her breast. He sat up, gazing at her with a hooded, scorching look that was as sexy as a caress.

Mesmerized, she watched as he tugged off his sweater and tossed it away, leaving his chest bare. Hastily he pulled her sweater over her head.

"Nick."

"Shh," he whispered, cupping her breasts. "You're beautiful, Grace. So gorgeous," he added, leaning down to kiss her breast. His wet tongue circled her nipple and she gasped, closing her eyes, clinging to him while she ran one hand over his muscled chest.

Pleasure rocked her in waves, heightening desire as he could so easily do. He tilted her back against his shoulder while he kissed her on the mouth and his hand slipped low again, going beneath her silk panties.

His warm fingers touched her intimately and she moaned as she arched against his hand, momentarily yielding, taking pleasure in touching him and being touched, knowing she was sinking deeper in her relation with Nick with each second that ticked past, each caress that bound her closer.

"Nick, wait. We're going way too fast and heading for intimacy, seduction, something I absolutely can't deal with," she said, pulling away.

His hot gaze traveled over her bare breasts and she couldn't stop doing the same, with a seeking study of his strong shoulders and chest. Her insides heated, clutched, an ache throbbing low inside her.

With an effort, she lifted her gaze. "Nick, slow down." She wiggled away, standing and pulling her sweater on, tugging her slacks back in place and fastening them.

Nick gripped her wrist. "Grace, come here."

"Didn't you hear me?" she asked as he pulled her toward his lap.

"Sit here with me. Let me talk."

Suspecting that if she sat on his lap they would do little chatting, she still did as he asked, tense and ready to protest the minute he started to kiss her. She was intensely aware of his bare chest, which kept her tingly and wanting him. Lust was rampant. How long could she successfully resist Nick? How badly would it complicate her life if she yielded to him?

"I want to tell you something. My dad does not give up easily," Nick said, and she chilled, fear overcoming desire.

"He's put me in a bind over Michael. If you legally changed Michael's last name, it would not give him to my dad."

"It would be a step in that direction and I don't think your dad will stop there. Do you really think so?"

"I can't imagine that he would ever try to take Michael from you. Especially after getting to know you. My father is not a monster. He's just a man who's determined to get his way when he wants something."

"And he wants Michael with all his being. He has nothing else to focus on in his life now. All his attention is on Michael and wanting my baby to be a Rafford. There's only one real way for Michael to become a Rafford and that's to take Michael from me."

"That's not true. There's another way."

Seven

Dread filled her as she looked into his eyes. Whatever he suggested could not be anything she would want to do. It had to involve losing some of Michael in her life.

"What does your dad intend?"

"You're right that his main goal is to get Michael in the family. He thinks I can accomplish this, so he's put pressure on me because he knows he's helpless to do much."

Her trepidation grew. "I don't want to know, but I have to hear. What are you instructed to do?"

"Bring Michael into the family. At least with the Rafford name and a promise my father can share in his life. Dad threatened me if I didn't accomplish this. He's changed his will."

"Nick, this is so unfair. Your father is ruthless and you're going to be the same way," she said, moving off his lap and walking to her mantel to get some distance from him. A knot had formed in her throat and she had turned to ice. "All right.

Tell me about this new will and how your father has threatened you," she said, bracing for what had to be bad.

Her spirits sank as Nick related the terms his dad had given him. When he finished, they gazed at each other in silence. She rubbed her forehead.

"I can't believe he would take your inheritance in such a manner."

"Believe it. My father does what he has to when he wants something. I checked with his attorney, who had been told he could talk to me about the new will."

"So if I don't capitulate, you lose a fortune."

Standing, Nick yanked on his sweater as he crossed the room to her. "I've thought of a solution. Hear me out, because your first reaction is going to be an emphatic no."

"You're not reassuring me. All right, what is your idea?"

"Marry me. We'll have a marriage of convenience."

Shocked, she stared at him momentarily speechless. "You're right," she said finally. "My reaction is a very emphatic no. We're not in love, Nick. You're not a marrying man. What happened to what you said to me—you're a confirmed bachelor. I recall, 'My father has married enough to scare me from that forever.'"

"I'm suggesting a temporary union. It's a marriage of convenience, no deep emotional involvement on either of our parts, but beneficial to both."

"I think 'beneficial' would be describing what you and your dad get. I would gain nothing."

"Of course you would," Nick said quietly, moving a strand of hair behind her ear, his touch mildly distracting even though her attention was on what he was saying. "I'd make it worth your while because I'll inherit the bulk of my dad's estate. Michael will have a trust and as my wife, you would have money to take care of him in any manner you desire. You can have your restaurant. In addition, I'll pay you a million."

Another surprise jolted her. Her head spun at the thought of what Nick was offering. Her life and Michael's would be altered drastically. "It boggles my mind. I can't imagine that much money being mine. I've been poor my whole life until the last few years and that's been what I've earned by hard work. You see what a simple life I lead. I can't fathom living in the manner you're proposing, much less marrying you. It's worth that much to you to do this?" she asked, unable to grasp how Nick could be making her such an offer.

"My father is enormously wealthy. If I inherit, I'll be a billionaire."

"It's that important to you that you would lock yourself into a loveless marriage?"

"Yes, to you. A union with you isn't exactly a grim prospect, Grace. We have a hot chemistry between us. We could make this work. I'll remind you again, it's temporary."

She rubbed her forehead again. "Nick, my head spins. It's lust between us. There are so many questions about the marriage, much less thinking of the future and Michael and the money."

"Look, I don't want to lose Dad's fortune, I'll admit that. No, we're not in love, but frankly, Dad's health is very poor. He spent years just sleeping three or four hours a night, working on high-pressure deals, partying when he wasn't working. He hasn't taken care of himself and now he's paying a price. His doctors have talked to me. We won't be married forever and you'll come out of it well fixed, Michael taken care of, and you and Michael can lead your own lives."

"That sounds cold."

"Not too cold," he remarked drily. "You and I get along great except for this problem between us caused by my dad. Marry me, let me adopt Michael. That puts him in the Rafford family, but there is no earthly way Dad could or would take him from you if you're my wife."

"I suppose that's true," she said. "Not as long as I stay with you."

"Damn straight. If you don't like being married to me, we don't have to be in each other's faces. There's enough money to do as you please. I'll set up an allowance for you that will be generous and you can do what you want. Keep catering, open your restaurant, stay home with Michael—suit yourself. This will give me Dad's inheritance and give you what you've dreamed of in life. You'll achieve that goal of yours far sooner."

Nick's dark gaze compelled her to want to accept. She moved away from him to break the spell he spun just with his presence.

"Nick, that's a lot to think about. You have to give me some time."

"I will, but remember, time is important. Dad could have another attack or a stroke, and then the deal is off because it would be too late. I hate to be blunt about it, but that's the truth as presented to me by his doctors."

"You would be Michael's legal father," she said, turning to study Nick and wondering how good this would be for Michael.

"I'm glad you're considering Michael, too. While he's only a baby, he has a big stake in your decision. As my child, he would be my heir and I would support him until he's grown." Locks of black hair fell across Nick's forehead and a muscle worked in his jaw, another hint of the intensity of his feelings.

"Of course, I'm wondering what kind of father you'd be."

"I can't make promises about something I don't know about myself, but I've been surprised how much he's wiggled into my life. I enjoyed last night and today with him around. He has a way of winning you over, though it's effortless on his part."

"Yes, he does," she said, thinking about Nick's declaration.

"This marriage between us won't last and I have no inclination to take Michael from you. Michael would be my heir."

"At least you're honest and that's good." They stared at each other and she could feel the clash of wills and see the determination in Nick's expression. He crossed the room to her to place his hands on her shoulders.

"Marry me. It won't be bad and you know it. You'd get what you want. I'd get what I want. Dad gets what he wants. It will be good for Michael and there is no way on earth you'll lose your baby. Dad and I will just be more in your life than otherwise."

"More in my life? Nick, you and I would have an intimate relationship."

"I can't see that that would be bad," he said quietly, slipping his hand to her throat. "We're not in love, but sex promises to be great between us."

"I still can't imagine you suggesting this. You have a lot to lose."

"Not as much as I have to gain," he countered. "My bachelor freedom I can forgo for a while. Grace, once again, this is a temporary marriage. It's not a lifetime commitment."

"You're charming and sexy. You've told me what a confirmed bachelor you are. Suppose I fall in love with you?"

"Hopefully, if that happens, I'll fall in love with you. If I don't, that's one of the risks you take, but there aren't many other risks and people can survive breakups. At the moment we're not in love."

"Intimacy may lend itself to love. I know I can't be detached about someone I'm intimate with."

"Regard it as a risk. I think this marriage will be well worth your while for all the pluses there are."

"You know I can't possibly give you an answer now."

"I'll repeat, don't wait long. I can't see that you have much to lose and you have a world to gain for both you and Michael." Nick drew her into his embrace and leaned forward to kiss her.

She stood resisting him, her thoughts on his proposition, but then his mouth opened hers, his tongue thrust inside and her attention shifted to Nick. He kissed her passionately as if trying to win her over physically, a reminder of the strength of their attraction. Marriage, making love constantly, a million dollars, plus her restaurant. It spun in her thoughts, but his kiss drove away reason. In seconds passion encompassed her.

She wound her fingers in his hair again, standing on tiptoe to kiss him ardently. She ran her hands over him, slipping them beneath his sweater to caress his smooth back, trailing down to his narrow waist.

Nick stepped back, pulling off first his sweater again, and then hers. "This is good, Grace. We do well together." His gaze traveled to her breasts as he unzipped her slacks and let them drop. He unclasped her bra to push it away, cupping her breasts to caress her before kissing her.

His tongue was hot, wet as he circled a nipple and made her clutch his shoulders. In minutes he straightened to kiss her, holding her with one arm banding her waist while his hand caressed her inner thighs. She spread her legs slightly, giving him access.

"You're beautiful. Desirable," he whispered. "Awesome," he added, his words another caress that heightened her desire.

His hand slipped higher and he tugged away her panties before his fingers touched her intimately, stroking her while he continued to kiss her.

Her heart thudded violently and she could feel his heartbeat racing beneath her hand spread on his chest.

She moaned with longing, sliding her hand down, unfastening his pants to get them out of the way and feeling his washboard stomach. Minutes later she pushed away his tight briefs. She took his stiff rod in her hand to caress him.

Sensations showered her, heightening her response and longing. She tugged at his shoulders, spreading her legs wider for him. "Nick," she whispered before kissing him.

She wanted him and she was crossing a line where there would be no turning back. She was also on the verge of accepting Nick's marriage proposal and then they would be making love every night. She would not stop him tonight. If marriage loomed she wanted him now before she made her decision, yet deep in her heart, she was inclined to say yes to Nick and take the breathtaking proposition he offered. Say yes and gain the world for herself and for Michael.

Nick's kisses and caresses reclaimed her attention and she forgot his proposition as she clung to him and returned his passion.

"Are you protected?" he asked, and she leaned away slightly.

"No," she answered.

"I can take care of it." He kissed her again until she forgot about his question or their brief conversation. He swept her into his arms and carried her to place her on the sofa. Picking up his trousers, he removed his billfold, retrieving a packet in foil.

She watched him, marveling at his strong body, virile and fit. He returned to kneel to kiss her, starting at her feet and working his way up until he moved between her legs and let his tongue travel where his fingers had played.

"Nick," she gasped, her fingers tangling in his hair. His tongue dallied across her belly, drifting higher to give attention to each of her breasts, and then he moved over her to kiss her, his weight solid.

She kissed him until he shifted, kneeling between her

open legs. His gaze traveled deliberately over her. "You're stunning." She watched his strong, well-formed hands as he put on the condom and then he lowered himself to enter her, filling her slowly, causing her to arch to meet him.

"Nick." She cried his name again, pulling his shoulders closer, running her hand down over his broad back and his firm buttocks. She locked her long legs around him, in motion with him, carried on a spiral of passion.

Nick slipped an arm around her, holding her, kissing her as he thrust slowly and withdrew, setting her on fire with need.

"Love me," she cried, her hips arching against him. His control held and he continued to pleasure her until her pulse roared in her ears and nothing existed for her except Nick's body pleasuring hers.

Finally his control shattered. He pumped faster, Grace moving with him as her need reached a climax. Carried high, she crashed with satisfaction that washed over her. She held him tightly while he shuddered with his release. His body was sweat covered, as heated as hers.

With a galloping heart, she gasped for breath until he kissed her passionately again, moving with her, slowing now. His breathing was heavy, irregular as her own.

"Nick, how I wanted you." She could never go back to feeling remote from him the way she had before.

"Ah, Grace, you're unbelievable, better than I had hoped, and I expected the world. We'll be great. You can't argue that one," he whispered, showering light kisses on her face while he held her. "This is a Christmas to remember. Make it extraordinarily special. Be my Christmas fiancée."

Christmas fiancée. How tempting Nick could be.

Slowly she cooled and caught her breath while she remained locked in his embrace, one with him and for now, no dissension between them.

"I want you in my bed every night. I would have without the proposal," Nick said, studying her, and her heart missed a beat over the promise of passion in his eyes. In that moment, she was certain she would fall in love with him. Particularly if he turned out to be a great father to Michael.

She combed raven locks off his forehead and Nick leaned down to kiss her. "Say yes, Grace. It'll be good for everyone. You won't have regrets."

"I'll have a hundred second thoughts and possibly dissatisfaction," she said, certain she would. "But I'll admit, I'm considering your proposal because Michael and I would gain. And it would keep your father from ever taking Michael away from me. I don't think a court would take a baby from the guardian mother, but I'm not a blood relative and your dad is. Plus he has the power and the money to win what he wants. He probably knows judges and has the best attorneys, whereas I can't possibly have the resources to put up much of a fight."

"Lamentably for you, that's right. My dad knows he can get what he wants." Nick rolled over, holding her tightly and keeping her with him as they squeezed together on her sofa.

"Next time we find a bed," he said.

"I have two bedrooms. One is empty now."

"That sounds promising. Can that be an invitation for me to stay?"

She smiled, tracing his lips with her fingers. "I suppose it is since you asked. Nick, I want to talk to my attorney about this."

"Fine. I had a prenup drawn up. It's in the car, so I'll get it before I leave. You can look at it and make changes, but everything you'll get is in the document."

"You're so sure of yourself, it's revolting," she said. "You already have the prenup. Your arrogance has always been obvious."

"But adorable," he said in fun. "I'm sure of myself because

this is a good deal. Grace, I don't give up my bachelor freedom lightly. I've thought about this."

"You want your inheritance as badly as your father wants Michael. Neither of you is accustomed to losing."

"You've managed to resist both of us pretty well so far. Frankly, I'd say you're the winner in this battle."

"Maybe I am," she said, winding her fingers in his chest hair and thinking about their lovemaking. "You're a sexy fellow."

He shifted to look down at her. "I'm glad you think so because you burn me to cinders."

"Ah, the result I intend," she said smugly, wishing with her whole heart she did. "Maybe I'll marry you and make you fall in love with me, you who are so sure of yourself."

He chuckled. "Do that. I'm not protesting. Let's go find your bed before one of us falls on the floor." When he stood and picked her up, she pointed in the direction of one of the open doors.

"I have a baby monitor in there and I can hear Michael anyway, although he rarely wakes in the night any longer."

"And which direction is the bathroom?"

"The door to the right," she said.

He placed her on the bed and brushed a light kiss on her mouth. "I'll be right back," he said, and left.

She stood, turned back the covers on the bed and climbed in, pulling a sheet over her. In minutes he returned, aroused and ready. He slipped in beside her and pulled her into his arms.

"Come here, sexy woman," he said, kissing her. His hand drifted down her back and over her bottom, rekindling desire.

It was dawn when she fell asleep in his arms. She had no idea how long she slept, but she stirred and looked at Nick, who had his arms wrapped around her as he held her close.

The past two days had been unforgettable, tonight's proposition, a shock. She would call her attorney to make sure the sham marriage would be as big a protection of Michael as Nick had said. She suspected it would because she couldn't imagine that it wouldn't completely satisfy Eli and return Nick's inheritance to him.

The risk was falling in love—inevitable with Nick. Would he ever really fall in love with any one woman? Or would he be in and out of marriages and relationships like his father?

One million dollars. Plus Michael taken care of financially for the rest of his life. Plus an allowance. She could not possibly refuse him. With her eyes adjusted to the darkness, she looked at Nick, seeing his handsome features, the thick midnight hair tumbling on his forehead, black lashes feathered over his cheeks.

Their lovemaking had been one more argument on Nick's side. The passion was fantastic, beyond anything she had dreamed possible. She studied Nick's straight nose and prominent cheekbones, his firm jaw. If Nick stayed in her life, she would fall in love—it was absolutely unavoidable. Yet heartbreak was a risk worth taking for everything else Nick promised. She just had to remember to not expect any long-term relationship. A temporary marriage with myriad benefits.

On any given day there were people walking around who were survivors of a broken heart. She would also pull through. He had a prenuptial agreement already drawn up, which was a clear indication of his confidence.

Her life was about to be turned topsy-turvy by the man holding her close. He was still a stranger in many ways, yet she was becoming friends with Nick, getting to know his father and learning some of the family history.

While she gazed at him and thought about their lovemaking, desire returned. Soon he had to be going, but they could make love one more time. She raised slightly to trace the curves of his ear with her tongue.

Almost instantly his arm tightened around her and his eyes opened. She gazed into his dark eyes and felt his arousal as he pulled her closer to kiss her and they loved once again.

It was the first graying of morning when she watched Nick dash to his car and return with a manila envelope. Once he closed the door he handed the envelope to her. "Look it over and give it to your attorney. I'll see you later today. Do you work or stay home?"

"Parties start up today and I'm working tonight. You can come by my office Monday at four and we can talk there."

They stood looking at each other. His warm brown eyes made it obvious he wanted to make love again. "You need to go, Nick. I have to get things done."

He stepped forward to embrace and kiss her. She hugged him tightly until finally she looked up. "You're a lusty one."

"You drive me to lust," he said, caressing her throat. "A few more minutes and we'll be back in bed. All right. I'll be at your office at four." He walked to his car and was gone. She closed and locked the door and went to look at Michael, studying the sleeping baby and thinking about how his life had changed.

She picked up the manila envelope to read the agreement, receiving more surprises with Nick's generosity, because she would get more than he had told her. Michael would have a trust that would assure him a college education and a comfortable life not counting contributions from her. She would be given a generous allowance, one million to be paid, half when they married and half when they separated. She paused at that one, certain that if she married Nick she wouldn't want it to end. She would do everything in her power to make him love her in return.

Michael's cries interrupted her reverie. She slipped the

agreement back into the envelope and it was midmorning before she had a chance to talk to her attorney. She drove to his office for an early afternoon appointment that was brief because he urged her to accept Nick's offer if she got along with Nick and thought she could live with him.

She drove back to the office and told Jada that she didn't want to be disturbed for the next hour while she sat in her office mulling over what she was about to do.

Nick arrived promptly at four. Jada, bubbling as ever around him, showed him back to Grace's office. She hadn't told Jada or anyone else except her attorney about Nick's proposal. This was something she wanted to make up her mind about without other influences except a legal opinion.

Nick walked in, his navy jacket unbuttoned and open. He closed her office door and crossed the room to kiss her, a light kiss that turned into a passionate one.

"Nick, we're in my office," she said finally, trying to catch her breath.

"With the door closed. It's private and you're delectable."

They studied each other and he raised one black eyebrow. "Did you talk to your attorney?"

"Yes. He gave me the go-ahead from a legal standpoint."

"Terrific. Now it's whether you want to live with me and take my offer or not." He embraced her lightly. "Will you marry me, Grace?" he asked, and she wondered if the day would come when she would wish those words had been said in love.

"Yes, Nick, I will. And I want the prenuptial agreement."

"Ah, Grace." He let out his breath and pulled her up to kiss her hard, an exuberant, triumphant kiss that started fires and made her want to be alone with him. He wrapped his arms around her to kiss her thoroughly, holding her close. She was committed now and her life had just changed forever.

He released her. "We need to get together to make our

plans. One thing—let's wed as soon as possible. I'll help you in every way I can and I'll pay for the wedding so spend what you want."

"Nick, slow down," she said, laughing as his words spilled out.

"I'm excited about this. When can you go with me to tell my dad?"

"Nick, won't he see right through this and know it's a sham marriage?"

"Not at all. He proposed to my third stepmother after knowing her a week. I've been in touch with him and he knows I see you. He'll accept it because it's what he wants. Michael will legally be his grandson. When can you get away to see him? Can you give me time tomorrow afternoon?"

"I have a wedding tomorrow night, but I'll turn things over to Jada and if you'll be here promptly at five, we can go then."

"I'll tell him today. I'll break the news so it's not too much of an emotional upheaval. He'll want to see you."

"I won't be able to stay long."

"That's fine. It shouldn't take long. He'll probably want a party sometime if the doctor allows it. We can do that after the wedding. So how soon can we get married?"

"I haven't thought ahead about this because I've spent my time trying to decide whether my answer would be yes or no. I don't have to have a big wedding. I just have Jada and another close friend, my two sisters, and my aunt."

"You know a lot of people because of your business and I imagine you have some clients you've gotten to be friends with. My dad is going to want the world to know about Michael. Between Dad's friends and mine, we'll have a big guest list."

"Why didn't this family feel that way about Michael when Alicia was alive?" Grace couldn't keep from saying, thinking what a sad turn of events to have them want Michael now after Alicia was gone.

"That was Bart's doing and I've told you, Dad's illness has changed his values. I'm giving you carte blanche to hire people and get everything pulled together quickly."

"How quickly? I want Aunt Clara to be a part of all this and she won't be back for two more weeks."

"Look at the calendar. Mid-January."

"You don't adopt Michael until we're married and I have the first half of my money," she stated firmly. "I've written that in the prenuptial agreement."

Amusement flashed in Nick's eyes. "Fine. Get your calendar. Friday is the last day of December. Let's have a wedding two weeks from that—it would be mid-January, actually almost three weeks away from today. Your aunt will have returned by then."

"Nick, this makes my head spin. Two weeks from this Saturday and a big wedding. My sisters may be in Timbuktu. We are so scattered."

"You contact them and let's get started. When can I have an evening with you?" he asked, his tone changing. Her pulse skipped and she wriggled away to look at her calendar. "Thursday is a rehearsal dinner that Jada can manage. I'll go out with you on Thursday."

"Great. Here," he said, handing her a credit card. "Use this. I'll have my secretary text the names of florists I've used a lot. If you trust me and will tell me what kind of music you like, I can get the musicians."

"Nick, we're doing this and we know so little about each other."

"We know what's important," he said, his expression changing. "I've thought about you all day long," he said. "I couldn't wait to see you," he added, and leaned close to kiss her again.

Wedding plans were forgotten, along with the tingly excitement she felt over her new life.

Desire overwhelmed her and she kissed him, letting go plans and worries. As their kisses heated and longing intensified, she wanted so much more. Reluctantly, she stopped.

"Nick, there's something else. I'd like to wait until we marry to have sex again. Last night was impulsive. I couldn't resist you and your seductive lovemaking. I don't rush into things and I'm charging headfirst into this marriage, definitely the physical relationship. Can we postpone sex until the wedding?"

"I'm not going to like waiting. What's the point?"

"A relationship now and getting ready for a crash wedding. These things will complicate my life at a time of the year when I'm really busy with my business. Plus if I stop working and stay home with Michael—which I will be able to do—I'll be busy getting the catering business taken care of," she said, thinking she was capitulating too fast to everything Nick wanted. He could wait for a physical relationship until the wedding. She didn't want to wait herself, but she wasn't going to be that easy for Nick.

"Whatever you want," he said. "Won't be agreeable, but if it's what you want, we wait."

"Thanks."

"No complaints over last night, are there?" he asked, studying her.

"What do you think?" she asked, running her hand along his thigh. He inhaled deeply and pulled her close.

"When you do that, I'm not keeping hands off," he said before he kissed her. Again, she responded, kissing him with abandon for a few more minutes, wondering whether she could resist him until they said vows. She intended for him to really desire her and she hoped above all, to avoid having him tire of making love before they became man and wife. Last night had been spectacular, fireworks and dizzying sex for her, but she didn't know if he had been as dazzled as she.

Now she poured herself into her kiss, on fire with longing, erotic images of Nick's virile body taunting her.

When she ended their kisses, she caught her breath. "I'm going to have to leave the office shortly for a party we're catering tonight. This is a large, important party and Glenda is keeping Michael for me."

"All right, I'll go. I'm going to miss you."

"Good. I want you to miss me," she said softly, tapping his chest and leaning closer to him. "I want you to miss me and think about me and count the minutes until we're together again."

"I think your wish is granted." He framed her face. "You've given me a fortune with your agreement. I'll make this marriage good for you in return. I just want to let Dad know and I want to have the ceremony as quickly as we can. Then I want to make love to you all night and all day long for at least a two-week honeymoon."

"Sounds wonderful, Nick," she said. "In your past relationships, I'm curious, have you always been the one to walk or have you ever had heartbreak?"

"No heartbreak, Grace. Either I've been the one or it's been mutual. Don't worry about when we part. We haven't gotten together yet."

She smiled at him. "You want this to be great and I do, too. Maybe our marriage will work the way we both hope," she said, wishing again that if she fell in love with him, it would be mutual and he would love her in return.

"What if I ask your father to escort me in place of my dad who's no longer living? Will that be too difficult for him? I really don't have anyone to ask. Clara's sons aren't close to me—I doubt if they'll even attend. Alicia's parents are gone, too. She had fewer relatives than I do, hence I have Michael."

"I'll check with Megan, but I doubt if it will be too hard for Dad. He can hang on to you. He will be overcome with delight that you asked him. You'll see—he will show his gratitude to you in some tangible way for the marriage and for asking him to escort you."

"I don't need that," she replied, and Nick shook his head.

"You're unique, Grace. Stop resisting accepting something good."

"You got what you want. I'm going to marry you. Now you go."

He smiled. "I'll go, but I'll be back and I will think about you while we're apart."

She walked to the front door with him, stepping outside where a chilly wind buffeted her. "I'll wait to tell anyone except Aunt Clara and my sisters until we've told your dad."

"Good."

Nick climbed in his car to drive away and she went to her office to call her aunt.

How would Clara react?

Eight

Nick called his father's house and let Megan know he was coming to the house to see his dad. The next call was to Jake and one to Tony, arranging to meet them at the club where they could eat. He called Jake's brother and asked Gabe to join them. With excitement humming in him, Nick drove away, thinking about the wedding. He would have to decide which of his friends he would ask to be in the wedding party. Tony and Jake definitely. Gabe would have to be included, perhaps as an usher. Who would be best man? He might have to flip a coin, but if he decided in such a manner, he would tell Jake and Tony when he was with both of them. The fortune was his. He had won over Grace. He'd lose his bachelor freedom—the minute he thought about the prospect, he remembered making love to Grace and became aroused. He wanted her constantly. He didn't mind losing his freedom if it meant sex constantly with Grace.

Except no sex until the wedding. Seemed silly to him

because she obviously wanted him and she was the sexiest woman he had ever been with. He couldn't concentrate on work today and too much of the time he had daydreamed about a honeymoon with Grace, something he hadn't given a thought to until after last night.

At his father's mansion, he went to the library and found his dad reading. His father looked up from his book. "To what do I owe this visit?" he asked. "You don't usually appear at this time of day."

"I can't stay long. I stopped by because I have some news that I think you'll like."

"Good. Maybe I can guess. I hope this involves my grandson. Grace has agreed to the name change."

"Better than that," Nick stated, his satisfaction increasing. "You know Grace and I have been seeing each other. Dad, I proposed and Grace has accepted. We're going to be married."

"I'll be damned," Eli said. A rewarding smile wreathed his face and Nick's spirits climbed another notch. "I hoped that might happen, but didn't think it would. Nick, this is the best news. You did it. Michael will be your child and you can adopt him."

"Grace has already agreed to the adoption."

"This won't be a long engagement, will it?" his Dad asked, squinting his eyes at Nick who smiled.

"No. We're definitely doing this—Saturday, January fifteenth."

"Excellent! You'll have to take time to have a drink with me now while I celebrate. You should have brought Grace," Eli said. His tone of voice had strengthened, sounding more like his former self.

"She wanted to come, but she had a party lined up. We'll both be here late afternoon tomorrow."

Nick poured two glasses of wine, taking one to his father, who stood to accept it.

"Tomorrow night we'll have champagne. I'm pleased beyond measure. I'll call about my will as soon as you leave. The bulk of my estate will go to you because now Michael will be your heir and it will pass to him someday."

"Thanks, Dad."

"Here's to success and a marriage that gives you tremendous joy. You did it, son. I knew you could." He raised his glass in a toast and Nick clinked his glass lightly against his dad's, then sipped his wine.

His father lowered his glass. "I like Grace, also."

"Of course you do. You like beautiful women."

His father chuckled. "This is a night to celebrate. I'll have to tell Megan the news."

Nick spent a leisurely hour with his dad and Megan before heading to the club to meet his closest friends.

When he joined Tony and Jake at their table in the bar, Jake frowned. "You look like the cat that swallowed the proverbial canary. What gives?" Jake groaned and slapped his hand against his face. "Aye-aye-aye. I'll bet I know why you wanted to see both of us. You did it?"

"Yes, I did,"

"Will you two stop the riddle and tell me what is going on?" Tony asked. "Oh, hell, I bet I know, too. Jake told me you were thinking about proposing to your caterer because of your dad. That's what this is about, isn't it?" Tony asked.

"You're exactly on target. Grace accepted my proposal."

"No surprise there," Tony remarked in a cynical tone. He stared at Nick. "You're loco and desperate to do this. Can't blame you. All three of us have manipulative dads. Whatever Eli threatened, he would carry it out, including cutting you off."

"It's a bummer and I hope you don't get hurt or aren't too miserable."

Nick smiled. "You've both seen Grace. I don't expect to be miserable one minute."

His friends stared at him, heightening his amusement over their glum reactions.

Just then, Gabe joined them. "Evening. Sorry I'm late. Have I missed anything?"

"Only that Nick is getting married," Jake drawled. "A damn marriage of convenience."

"You might hold the congrats," Tony said. "Unless you want to congratulate him for getting his inheritance."

"Sorry, no congratulations here. I'm surprised you look as happy as you do, because you just lost one million in that bet you three made."

"I've already heard about that," Nick said, smiling at them.

"You're loco. You're smiling when you've lost a million, you're getting a loveless marriage and you will be a dad overnight. You know nothing about babies," Tony said.

"I'll manage."

"He's lost his mind," Tony said, and the others agreed while Nick took some more good-natured kidding.

"You're not scared or worried about this marriage, are you?" Jake asked.

"I'm not thrilled with what I have to do, but scared or worried to have a marriage of convenience with Grace and inherit my father's fortune? No. I think this is going to work."

Jake looked at Tony and they both nodded. "He's done it," Tony said.

"So we might as well accept the inevitable and toast him on succeeding in getting back his inheritance. That would have been a hell of a loss," Jake said. All three men raised glasses and Nick raised his to touch each glass lightly.

"Here's to success, Nick, and a rewarding bargain with Grace."

"Thanks for the grudging wishes," Nick said and sipped his martini. As he lowered his glass, Gabe stood. "I'm meeting a friend for dinner. I'll see you guys later. Congratulations, Nick."

"Thanks, Gabe. Keep in mind, the wedding is mid-January."

"You're not wasting any time," Tony remarked as Gabe walked away.

"Nope, I'm not. There's no reason to and that's the first question from Dad—he wanted to make certain this wasn't a long engagement. He's talking to his attorney about his will as we speak. Now, will both of you be able to be there?"

As soon as they gave him affirmative answers, Nick set down his glass to get a quarter from his coat pocket. "Okay. I can't choose between my lifelong closest friends, so I'll flip a coin for best man unless one of you definitely doesn't want the task."

Again his friends exchanged a look and then Jake shrugged.

"Flip away, but you won't hurt feelings if you make the choice without the coin. We're too close and have been that way for too long to get bent out of shape. Especially after offering to flip."

"We'll flip first to see who calls it." Nick flipped and the two men looked at each other waiting a second before Jake spoke. "Tails."

They looked down at the coin. "Tony gets to call this time for best man." Nick tossed the coin in the air.

"Tails," Tony said as the quarter dropped to the table.

"It's heads. Jake, you're my best man if you want to be."

"Sure. Thank you. I'm honored."

"So am I even though I lost," Tony said.

"So we'll have another drink on me to say goodbye to your freedom. You have three weeks to back out. You really don't have to have the money," Jake said.

"Oh, yes, I do. I'm not letting that fortune get away. You two will marry in the next few years, so stop grousing over my marriage."

"We're not marrying in the next few years. I don't plan to ever," Jake said firmly.

"I don't until I'm fifty. By then I'll have enough sense and experience to continue to avoid the marriage trap," Tony said.

"You cynical guys," Nick said good-naturedly. "I'll be astounded if one of you isn't married or planning to marry before next year is up."

"No way," Tony protested.

"Just watch us," Jake added.

"I will watch." Nick grinned. "How about we order dinner now?" he asked, and their conversation shifted to basketball. He tried to pay attention though his thoughts constantly returned to Grace.

The first morning Clara was back in town, she went to Grace's house to keep Michael. As she held Michael and Grace finished her coffee, Clara sat at the kitchen table and put Michael in a high chair to feed him breakfast.

"Grace," she said, and dread filled Grace. "Why are you marrying Nick? When I left town before Christmas, you were totally against an arrangement like this."

Grace looked into eyes as green as her own. "I could tell you it was a whirlwind courtship and we both fell in love, but I think you'd know that's not the truth. It's a marriage of convenience. I'll get a lot out of agreeing."

"No!" Clara said, looking down at Michael.

"Wait until you hear Nick's proposition," Grace urged, and related Nick's offer to her aunt.

Clara stared at Grace with her mouth open for a moment. She seemed to realize what she was doing and her mouth snapped closed. "A million dollars," she whispered. "Grace, if he adopts Michael and then divorces you, he can sue for full custody and as the father, he will stand a chance. With his resources, he can hire more and better lawyers than you can. You may lose Michael."

"Nick isn't after Michael. He wants his father's inheritance. He has no desire to take Michael from me. He is a confirmed bachelor and not into kids or marriage. He's looking at this as a temporary arrangement."

"His father may live for years."

"We'll face that as time passes."

"You've had a complete turnaround since I left town." Clara's eyes narrowed. "Grace, have you fallen in love with Nick?"

Grace looked down at her hands in her lap. "I might be on the verge of it," she answered quietly.

"You have. Has he declared love for you?"

"No, or it wouldn't be a marriage of convenience."

"No, it wouldn't. You'll get hurt in this. He'll break your heart when he walks out of your life. And he may break Michael's, too."

"Frankly, from the way he talks about his father's health, I don't expect Nick to be around long enough for Michael to form that strong an attachment. He's a baby and he won't remember Nick clearly."

"A million dollars and Michael taken care of financially. Plus you'll have an allowance, a new car, clothes, all sorts of things." Clara sighed. "I suppose I can't blame you, but I'd hate to see you get hurt."

"Maybe I can make him fall in love with me," Grace replied quietly.

"Don't count on any such dream happening," Clara said. "The world is filled with brokenhearted women who've had that dream."

"I know you're right."

"I suppose I would do the same thing if I were you," Clara admitted. "I doubt if either of my boys can get here for your wedding."

"That's all right. It's not like it's the real thing. I keep thinking of this as a business arrangement," she said, knowing she didn't altogether. Grace smiled. "I'll have enough money to buy you a house close to us."

"Have you considered what you'll do about your business?"

"I'm keeping my catering business for the time being, but I'll turn the running of it over to Jada most of the time. I'll begin working at home, making plans for a restaurant because now that can actually happen. I promise, you'll get to keep Michael plenty."

"I suppose, but I'm going to worry about you going into a loveless marriage no matter how much he bribes you to do it. I can't blame you for what you've done, though. That's too much money to turn down. I just hope it protects Michael for you. Have you told your sisters?"

"I did and they're coming for the wedding. They'll be bridesmaids."

"Are they excited over the man you're marrying?"

"Doreen and Tanya don't know Texans. They don't have any idea who Nick Rafford is. I just told them he's a Dallas oilman and let it go at that."

"They will be beside themselves when they find out. Your sisters both like men with money."

Grace smiled. "I want you there for the wedding."

"Of course."

"I can fly Chet and Miles here should they want to come. Nick is paying for everything. If you can, I'd like you to go with me tomorrow when I shop for my wedding dress."

Clara shook her head again. "You're moving way too fast. I'll have to get a dress, too. And we'll have to get Michael a tux—a baby in a tux," she said, and Grace laughed. "I suppose we can dress him in a suit," Clara added.

"He'll have a tux," Grace said. "Right now, nothing seems real about the marriage or the wedding ceremony."

"The middle of January will come soon."

Enchanted, Grace looked around the huge ballroom of Eli's mansion. A fire blazed in a massive stone fireplace while an orchestra played and she danced in Nick's arms.

"I can't believe I'm here in your arms and I've had an enormous wedding with hundreds of guests. This is a dream come true."

"I'll say that about eight hours from now," he said.

"Or sooner if we can," she added breathlessly. The weeks since his proposal had been a dream—the excitement, the preparations, the presents, and in the center of it all was Nick. She had difficulty believing she was actually his wife now. Mrs. Nicholas Rafford.

Her life had turned upside down and at the moment she was deliriously happy as she looked into Nick's eyes. Whatever their future, today, as well as the next two weeks on a honeymoon with Nick, should be paradise.

"You're beautiful, Mrs. Rafford," he said. "And hot. You don't have any idea what you do to me."

"Thank you, my handsome, sexy husband. This is paradise."

"Oh, no. How wrong you are. Paradise will be tonight. That's when the fireworks begin. Hopefully a little sooner than that. If I could kiss you now the way I want, people would stare because it would not be a casual kiss."

"You won't hear any objections when we're alone. Oh, Nick, this is wonderful," she said.

He spun her around and watched her with a look of satisfaction. "This marriage may be the best merger and greatest idea I've ever had."

"Don't sound so smug," she said in amusement, and he grinned at her.

"I have a right to be smug. Marrying you, giving Dad what he wants, getting what I want, taking you on a two-week honeymoon—how could I possibly top that?"

He spun her around the floor and then the music changed to a fast Latin number and she danced, watching Nick, flirting silently and exchanging looks that heated her more than ever.

Finally she was back in his arms for another slow dance.

"How could your family know so many people?" she asked as they danced past others. "I'd guess fifty or seventy-five from my guest list are here. All the rest of this enormous crowd is from your dad's and your list."

"Dad has always led a social life, been active in business, been on boards. We know a lot of people. There's only one person I'm interested in today."

She gazed up at him, tingles tickling her as their gazes locked and she forgot the crowd. "Nick, I know we can't, but I'm ready to leave here."

He drew a long breath. "I'm thinking of all the things I want to do with you when we're alone," he said in a husky voice.

"You're making it harder."

"*Au contraire,* darling. You're the one making it harder," he said in a double entendre that caused her cheeks to burn as she smiled at him.

"I hope so," she replied softly.

"You better stop before I whirl you out of here, away from everyone, and make mad, passionate love to you."

"You tempt me," she said, flirting with him.

"Grace, one more minute and I carry out my threat."

"Very well, we'll be proper and perform our duties as the honorees." She looked at her hand on his shoulder, still dismayed by the enormous diamond ring he had given her. "My ring has to be the most spectacular ring in the world. Nick, it's worth a fortune by itself, not to mention the other things you've done for me," she said. She recalled how awed over the ring she had been when he surprised her with it, kissing her passionately and telling her how glad he was she'd accepted his proposal.

"I wanted you to have it and I'm glad you like it."

"It impressed my sisters," she said, and he grinned.

"I'm still doubtful if they're really your sisters. Bart and I weren't alike, but you and your sisters don't have a shred of resemblance in personality or looks."

She glanced around the room and spotted Doreen's platinum-blond hair. As usual, Doreen had a crowd of men around her. In seconds she saw Tanya, who had two men talking to her, her head tilted and her thick mane of raven hair hanging straight.

"We're not alike in any way. I'm surprised they came. They have been dazzled by you and your friends. I think they are enjoying themselves tremendously. To me, none of this seems real, except I know it is," she said, gazing up at the sexy, spellbinding man who had been her husband for a couple of hours.

"It is definitely real," he remarked. "You look gorgeous. I'd guess I've told you that a dozen times today."

"Thank you, my virile husband," she replied, thinking what a whirlwind the past week had been. The first half of the million-dollar payment had been transferred to her, divided up among savings, stocks, bank accounts and various investments that one of Nick's financial advisers had recommended. Michael had a trust fund now and already her life had been transformed. She owned an entire new wardrobe. She had handed off the running of the catering business to Jada. If successful and turning a profit, the catering business would be sold to Jada in six months.

While Nick spun Grace around the floor, she held his broad shoulder and his warm hand. "This is the most beautiful place and perfect for a reception."

"There have been lots of parties here." Nick glanced around. "I think we pass for a couple completely in love."

"I'm going to make you fall in love with me, Nick Rafford," she declared. His gaze returned to her, a warmer, more intense look this time.

"Today I am in love with you," he said lightly, and her heart missed a beat. She reminded herself that he answered without really meaning it, carried away by the moment and the prospects of the night before them and a honeymoon, but she meant what she had said to him. She danced with him, hoping the marriage did last, knowing she was falling in love with Nick whether he ever returned it or not.

"At the moment what I'm most interested in is when can we be alone?"

"Not for a few hours," she said. "Anticipation should make it better."

"No, it doesn't." He spun her around and then pulled her close for a moment. Desire was constant, intense, and she wanted to be alone with Nick. Instead, she gazed into his eyes, smiled and followed his lead around the dance floor.

Next Nick danced with Clara while several women took care of Michael. Eli appeared to ask Grace to dance as he had told her he would. It was a slow number and she was surprised that Eli was getting around better than he had any time she had seen him.

"This day is monumentally important to me, Grace," he said, smiling at her. "You've brought me great joy. I was deeply touched and honored to escort you down the aisle to give the bride away."

"I'm glad and I appreciate you walking with me," she said. "Thank you again for your extremely generous wedding gift to us," she said, thinking of the luxurious chalet in Switzerland he had presented to them, giving Nick keys and papers and showing them pictures.

"I have a gift for you when this dance is over. You've brought so much happiness into my life. I never gave my sons the attention I should have. I live with regrets now, but Michael gives me somewhat of another chance. I hope to have a close relationship with my grandson."

"You didn't need to give me a gift," she said, surprised because she barely knew Eli and couldn't imagine she would mean much to him. "And it'll be good for Michael to be close to his grandfather."

"I'm overjoyed also to see Nick marry. I had many marriages. My ex-wives have all remarried, so I rarely see them. Even so, marriage is good and I'm happy about Nick." The dance ended and Eli grasped her arm. "Come with me a moment," he said, motioning to Nick.

"Just a brief time with both of you. I have a gift for Grace." He led them to a small reception room and closed the door, muting the noise of the band and crowd.

He summoned a butler to bring the gift for Grace before turning to her. "Grace, you've given me enormous pleasure. Both of you have." She glanced at Nick as he took her hand. There was a light rap on the door and then a butler entered to place a large, beautifully wrapped box tied with a huge pink bow on a table. He left, closing the door behind him.

Surprised it was solely for her, she unwrapped it and raised the lid, moving away papers. She gasped as she looked at an oil painting in a gilt frame. Certain she was looking at an original Monet, she was awed. "My word, this is for me?" she asked, looking up at Eli.

"Yes, my dear. For sharing my grandson with me and for marrying my son," Eli said.

Stunned by his generosity, she brushed Eli's cheek with a kiss. "Thank you. You know I will treasure this painting and I hope someday it will be Michael's."

"Ah, that, too. That will be good," Eli said, reaching into his pocket and turning to Nick.

"I've changed my will and given you both a wedding present, but the gifts now are out of gratitude and happiness over your marriage and over Michael. Nick, this is for you," he said, handing a check to Nick. "Do what you want with it."

Nick looked down and then at his dad. He stepped forward to hug Eli. "Thanks, Dad. This is a generous gift. We both thank you." Nick showed her and she looked at a check for thirty million dollars.

Stunned by the size of the gift and the manner in which the two men were dealing with such a sum, she was breathless.

"Thank you, Eli. It's an overwhelming gift, just as your other gifts are," she said, wondering about the adjustments to her new lifestyle.

"We're both glad you're happy, Dad," Nick added, exchanging a satisfied look with his father.

"Now we better go back or our guests will think the bride and groom have left, the party is over and they'll go home. Grace, you can get your painting after your honeymoon. I'll keep it for you until then," Eli said, summoning the butler again.

Grace returned to the reception with Nick, but she walked

without seeing anyone or hearing the music. She was still wrapped in shock over the enormous gifts they had been given.

It was two hours later when Nick whispered in her ear, "What would it take to get you to leave with me now?" His brown eyes burned with desire.

"I thought you'd never ask," she answered.

His chest expanded as Nick took a deep breath and looked beyond her. "Everyone will understand if we don't say goodbye."

"Michael won't. I have to see him," she said.

Nick took her hand and in minutes she had kissed Clara and Michael. She left with Nick, hurrying to the waiting limo. As they sped to the airport and Nick's private luxury jet, he pulled her onto his lap to take her into his arms.

"We did it, Grace. I get what I want, including you, and you get what you want—a fortune, a secure future for Michael. He'll be a Rafford soon, legally my son with all the benefits and someday he'll inherit the Rafford fortune."

As Nick talked, she had a pang, wishing she was hearing words of love instead of the results of the contract they had signed. "We have a great business deal," she said. His intense gaze always saw too much, so she leaned closer to put her mouth on his.

The instant she kissed him, his arm tightened around her waist and he drew her closer. When he slipped his hand beneath her long skirt, her silk dress rustled. He caressed her inner thigh, his touch light yet searing.

Desire consumed her. She wanted to shove away his jacket and his shirt, to touch and kiss him. She tore her mouth from his. "How long before we're where it's private?"

His hungry expression intensified and he glanced beyond her, closing the partition between them and the driver. "We have a little time."

Pulling up her silk skirt, she pushed him down on the smooth leather seats and straddled him while she unbuttoned his shirt. Her tongue trailed down his chest, circling his flat nipples, inching across his muscled belly.

He was aroused, straining against his tux trousers and she ran her hand over him lightly. He groaned, sitting up and pulling her to him as he kissed her. His tongue thrust into her mouth while his hand slipped beneath the neckline of her dress.

After a few minutes, she slid off his lap and gripped his wrists. "We wait. The limo will arrive at the airport and when the door is opened, I want to be ready to step out."

Nick was breathing hard, desire obvious in his dark gaze that peeled away the wedding dress, but he began buttoning his shirt. "Soon," he said.

She straightened her dress and sat beside him, watching him get his clothes in place. They exchanged a look that made her temperature climb another notch and then he leaned close to brush her lips with a light kiss. "This is taking all kinds of self-control."

"Just think about that door opening shortly and that you have to get out and talk to your pilot and others."

Nick smiled at her and pulled her onto his lap. "I can hold you until we get there."

Feeling giddy, she combed his hair back in place with her fingers. She leaned close to trace his ear with her tongue. "I can barely wait, too, Nick," she whispered in his ear, blowing her warm breath on him. "I'll kiss you from head to toe."

"Grace," he said in a rough, husky voice, turning to kiss her until the limo slowed.

She slipped off Nick's lap quickly and straightened her clothes. "Nick, my hair—"

"Is beautiful and I will soon take the rest of it down," he

said as the limo door opened and they stepped outside. She had envisioned a small jet. Instead, it looked like a commercial airliner.

The moment she stepped on board, she wondered just how much her new husband was worth. "Nick, this is a palace," she said, surprised by the sumptuous luxury of the cushioned seats, the small bar and big-screen television. She had given her clothes to Nick, who had had them delivered early to the plane so she could change out of her wedding dress after boarding.

"We'll have to buckle up until we're airborne and the flight is smooth. Then we can move around," Nick said, leading her to a seat.

She sat near him and fastened a buckle over her lap. "I could change first."

He shook his head. "Wait. It won't be long."

She watched out the window when they lifted and circled above Dallas to head northeast.

Once they had leveled off and were airborne, she gazed out at a cerulean sky dotted with a few small clouds. The dreamlike feeling continued to capture her. The entire ceremony had seemed imaginary. Now this flight on a plane that was fit for a king was also like a dream.

"A perfect day, a dream night," Nick said, brushing her knuckles with a kiss and holding her hand.

"It was a perfect day. This brief time together was the closest I've felt to my sisters. Maybe it was just an age difference thing when I was growing up. I really enjoyed them today and I think they'll come back to visit."

He chuckled. "I think they decided they like some of the men they've met. Tanya told me she's flying to Houston to go out with Todd Deakins."

"He's one of your friends. I don't know him, but she told me she'd met someone she was going to see again."

Nick unbuckled his seat belt. "You can unbuckle now," he said, taking her hand. "Let's get you out of that dress."

"Actually, I may need help with the buttons. Aunt Clara got me into this."

"And I will take great pleasure in getting you out of it. While you are gorgeous in it, you are breathtaking without it, so without it wins," he said.

She drew a deep breath when they entered a plush bedroom. "What don't you have on this plane?" she asked, turning to look at him, her thoughts of the plane vanishing instantly at the look in Nick's eyes.

"The most important thing this plane has today is you," he said in a husky voice, drawing her to him. "We're alone in here, undisturbed unless there's some flight turbulence."

"Hopefully, the only turbulence will be in that bed," she drawled. "Come here, Nick," she whispered, standing on tiptoe to kiss him.

Something flashed in the depths of his dark gaze before she closed her eyes as they kissed and their tongues touched. She tingled, desire enveloping her with urgency.

"I want you more than I've ever wanted anyone in my life," he said, combing his fingers in her hair. "I can't get you out of my thoughts. I'm going make love to you all through this honeymoon. You drive me wild, Grace," he whispered, showering kisses on her and then turning her around.

His breath was warm on her nape and she felt his fingers twisting free the buttons of her dress. She reached behind her to place her hands on his thighs. "Hurry with those buttons, Nick. I can't wait."

"I'd like to tear it off you."

"Oh, no. Not my wedding dress."

He trailed kisses down the row he had opened in the back of the dress. She wore no bra beneath it and in minutes it fell around her ankles, billowing with a soft hiss.

She turned, and he caught her as she reached for him, holding her a few inches away to look at her, a heated look that made her tremble with longing.

"Nick," she said, taking off his shirt and unfastening his trousers, letting them fall. He stepped out of them to rid himself of the rest of his clothes, and she studied him as hotly as he seemed to be looking at her. He was virile, sexy, ready for love, with a lean, muscled body.

Reaching for her, he pulled her into his embrace. "Mrs. Nick Rafford, I'm going to kiss you all the rest of this day and night."

"I want to make you fall in love and never want to walk away," she admitted. She received a hooded look from him that burned with desire, and she wondered if her words had registered with him.

"You're gorgeous," he said before placing his mouth on hers, and she forgot the future and vows and their contract marriage.

After making love throughout the night and next day, they flew to a villa Nick had leased in the south of France, where the beach was a perfection of white sand and blue water. She never was on the beach.

Late one afternoon as she reclined in his arms on a chaise near their pool after making love, she toyed with his chest hair, curling it around her fingers. "Nick, this is paradise."

"It is paradise, indeed," he said in satisfaction.

"We go home tomorrow."

"I'd like to extend our honeymoon, but I have to get back. We'll try to get away together next month. How's that?"

"It's fine. We might as well not travel so far. We could be fifty miles from Dallas for all we've been out of the bedroom."

He chuckled. "If you knew what the lease for this villa

cost, you would know it's far more than anything fifty miles from Dallas."

"I hope we can return sometime and I can look around, because I suspect it's beautiful."

"I haven't noticed anything except you," he said, kissing the inside of her wrist. "This is the best, Grace. You're all I want. This marriage is the smartest thing I've ever done. It's given us each other."

"Talk, talk, talk," she whispered, really loving every word yet knowing he had different thoughts in his head about their union than she. She kissed him and their conversation ended for the time being as Nick began to caress and kiss her in return.

Tomorrow they would return home, back to reality and problems and the future. Would Nick be as interested in her when they were in familiar surroundings?

She hugged him tightly while they kissed. Daily she fell more in love with him. Did he feel anything for her in return or was it all lust?

Nine

They returned home the last week of January and she moved into his condo with a suite containing an enormous master bedroom. Her first task was to redo the adjoining room into a nursery so Michael would be close at hand.

She went to the office twice a week, but the rest of the time was spent at home with Michael while decorators transformed the room into the new nursery. It was idyllic and after the passionate honeymoon, each night with Nick was paradise.

The last day of January, she bubbled with eagerness for Nick's arrival. She had bathed and dressed in new red pants and a red silk shirt. She was on the nursery floor with Michael, stacking toy plastic rings on a wide plastic peg when Nick entered the room.

"At last you're here," she said, coming to her feet to cross the room to kiss him. He pulled her close, kissing her long and thoroughly before releasing her because Michael was throwing blocks.

"I think I miss you more each day."

"I hope you do, because I miss you and can't wait for you to walk through that door."

"I can't wait for bed," he said, kissing her again. "Whoa," Nick said, abruptly ending his kiss and looking down at Michael, who was tugging on his pant leg and trying to pull himself up.

"Hey, fella." Nick bent to scoop up Michael "Are you wanting some attention, too?" he asked, swinging Michael up to kiss his cheek. "Have you been waiting for your dad to get home?"

She wondered how long it would take her to get used to hearing Nick refer to himself as Dad. It had been Nick's suggestion because he said he was legally going to become Michael's father. It suited her, but she hadn't grown accustomed to thinking of Nick as a dad. She had tried to teach Michael to say "dad."

Michael laughed and held out his small arms and Nick hugged him. He handed Michael to Grace. "Take him a minute and let me get out of this jacket and tie."

When she sat on the floor again and took Michael from Nick, she watched Nick shed his coat and tie. Wind had tangled his thick hair. He looked virile, energetic, sexy. She wanted to be in his arms and to make love, but Michael was awake and she needed to care for him and, shortly, feed him.

Nick dropped down beside her, brushing a light kiss on her mouth while Michael wiggled to get free. She set him down and he began to climb on Nick, who lay on the floor and swung Michael above his head, making Michael giggle.

"You're an easy one to please," Nick said to the baby while Michael babbled. He swung Michael to the floor and set him down, scooting back to roll a ball to him. Michael laughed and picked it up to try to chew on it.

"Hey, that's not what you do," Nick said, taking the ball. "When does he outgrow chewing on everything?"

"Probably when he has more teeth."

"That's going to be next year at the rate he's going," Nick said, and she smiled.

"The pediatrician said his teething is quite normal," she said. She had been surprised and pleased by how much Nick enjoyed playing with Michael. His attention to Michael seemed to grow steadily. She wondered if it was a deliberate effort on Nick's part to make her happy or if he truly enjoyed Michael.

"Your dad called today and I told him we would bring Michael to see him either this evening or tomorrow."

"We can go now. We can grab something to eat on the way. Dad will have already eaten." Nick continued to play with Michael, but he turned to smile at her. "I've thought about you all day. Let's go right now so we can come home early."

"Good plan, Nick," she said, thinking that he sounded like a man in love even if he didn't say he was. Or was she fooling herself? Nick seemed deeply interested in Michael. She prayed he was falling in love with her and that love for Michael was growing, real love that would make him want them all to stay together.

Nick stood and picked up Michael, carrying him to put on his jacket and place him in the carrier. She watched Nick bending over the baby, talking to him and Michael smiling at Nick.

"Da," Michael said, holding up his arms.

Startled, Nick glanced at her. "Did you hear him? He called me 'Da.'"

Surprised herself, she watched Michael as Nick picked him up again. "Da," Michael mimicked, playing with Nick's nose.

"Hey, he's calling me Dad," Nick said, grinning at her.

She placed her hand on her hip and stared at Nick. "I never thought I would see you happy about that," she said, amazed at Nick's reaction.

"I think it's great. I'm his dad now and will legally be for the rest of both of our lives whatever happens with you and me," Nick said, making cute faces at Michael and shaking his head, causing Michael to giggle.

Nick's casual "whatever happens to you and me" hurt. The marriage was still a temporary state in his mind, and it didn't sound as if he had given the slightest consideration to making it something lasting.

"You're turning into a good dad, Nick."

"It's easy with a cute baby like Michael."

"You enjoy being his dad."

"Sure. He's a cute little guy. Why wouldn't I care for him? He has my looks and maybe he'll act like I do."

"What an ego," she said playfully.

"Let's go so we can come home to bed," he said, slipping on his suit jacket while she went to get her coat. He helped her on with her coat and pulled her into his arms to kiss her.

As soon as he released her he picked up Michael. "Come on, Michael, we're going for a ride. Dad will take you to see Granddad."

Later, as Eli watched Nick playing with Michael, she sat quietly. Megan joined them now most times they visited and Grace had enjoyed getting to know Megan better. As she looked at Megan and thought about her being a nurse, Grace's nagging worry returned.

It was the end of January, time for her period. She had missed one at the end of December which she figured was because of the excitement and upheaval in her life. Occasionally she'd had late periods, but she had never missed two periods. A chill of concern slithered down her spine, but she tried to reassure herself. They had used protection. That first time it had been a condom and after that she had been on birth control pills. It had to be the enormous changes she had experienced. There was no real likelihood that she was pregnant and she felt fine.

She watched Nick sitting on the floor with Michael and laughing, causing Michael to laugh. When she glanced up at Eli, his face was wreathed in smiles. His hair was laced with white and he looked like a benevolent grandfather, not a ruthless entrepreneur.

He had been good to her, but then he had what he wanted from her. She had benefited, and would the rest of her life. She was beginning to lose the lingering hostility over Bart's treatment of Alicia. None of them had dealt directly with Alicia except Bart, so it was unfair to blame Nick or his dad, although Eli could have made Bart treat Alicia in a better manner as easily as he had caused Nick to end up in this marriage.

"Nick, you get to play with him every night at home. Bring me my grandson and let me hold him a minute before you go."

Talking to Michael, Nick carried him to Eli. Nick sat close at hand and stretched out his long legs, looking at her, and for a moment she felt closed off in a world with just Nick. He winked at her and then turned his head to converse with Megan, who had asked him a question.

In minutes, Nick stood and picked up Michael. "Dad, it's time to take him home. His charm will vanish when he gets sleepy."

"That is definitely not so," Eli protested with a smile. "I have never seen Michael fussy."

"Don't pin Grace down on that one. Michael has his moments, but all in all he is one happy fella," Nick said, putting Michael's jacket on him once again.

It was an hour before they were home and had Michael

tucked in his crib. She smoothed his mussed hair and touched his cheek lightly. "He's asleep," she whispered.

Nick stood beside her with his arm around her. "Little guy is worn-out."

Knowing he was asleep, they left the room where a small light burned. As she headed for the door, Grace looked appreciatively at the nursery. It was a dream compared to the simple room she had left behind.

In the darkened living area of Nick's condo, a fire burned in the fireplace and outside lights twinkled in a panoramic view of Dallas.

"At last, we're alone," Nick said, shedding his jacket and pulling her into his arms to kiss her. Her fingers went to the buttons of his shirt and in seconds she ran her hands over his chest as she kissed him.

Hours later, she fell asleep in his arms, holding him tightly and wondering where their relationship was headed and if Nick would ever move beyond lust. What would happen if she admitted she loved him?

Grace waited another week until the first of February. She had definitely missed the second period and her worries were growing. She couldn't imagine she was pregnant, but something was wrong. She made a doctor's appointment, but the day before the appointment, she bought a pregnancy kit.

While Michael napped, she tried it. Her head swam and her stomach knotted when she stared at the results. "I can't be," she whispered to no one. Dizzy, turning cold, she sat down and stared into space.

Then her emotions swung the opposite direction as she thought about having Nick's baby. *Another precious baby* was her reaction as she placed her hand on her stomach. Longing struck her. If only their marriage were real and Nick cared. What a joyous moment this would be. For an instant her spirits soared as she thought about another baby. And then they crashed into reality.

A pregnancy was not something they had given one thought to happening. Nick would feel trapped and angry. Certainty settled on her that he would want out of the marriage.

Her throat grew tight. Now there would be no chance for this fledgling relationship to grow into true love, become lasting or meaningful.

She couldn't imagine breaking the news to Nick. She placed her hand on her flat stomach. For all his joy with Michael, he was just on the fringe of becoming a dad. Another baby in his life—this baby would be his own—was not in his plan.

He had made it emphatically clear this was a marriage of convenience that would not last. He would not want the complication of a baby.

Clenching her fists, she contemplated the future. Whatever he did, he had his inheritance. Eli would not be happy with Nick if they separated, but given his own past, she was certain he would accept a split. Eli would love the news. This would be his second grandchild and Nick's baby. She had an ally in her father-in-law. He would celebrate. She was glad to think about Eli's joy in the event, but Nick's unhappiness offset any real delight she could feel over Eli's attitude.

She was not going to tell Nick yet. She wanted to see the doctor and have her pregnancy confirmed by an expert before she told anyone.

The next day she left Michael with Clara and at three in the afternoon, she kept her doctor's appointment.

The doctor confirmed that she was definitely pregnant, the baby due in September. Now she had to tell Nick.

That night she tried to look her most seductive. Clara was keeping Michael overnight and Grace had bought a new black lace teddy. She took a long, leisurely bath and dressed in the teddy, leaving her hair falling free. She had to fight the temptation to put off telling him because she had been in a magical paradise with Nick and she didn't want it to end. If only the pregnancy had occurred after at least a year with him, giving Nick time to fall in love with her—and Michael. She sighed.

The cook had prepared dinner. She had requested something special that would keep by letting it remain in a low oven.

She had given the staff time off and none of Nick's staff lived in his condo, so she and Nick would have the place to themselves. He called to tell her he would be home by six.

Her anticipation heightened as the time drew close. And then she heard the locks click free. She went to the front door wearing only the teddy and high-heeled black sandals.

Nick was just inside the front door when she stepped into the wide marble-floored entryway.

"Welcome home," she said, hoping her voice sounded sultry.

Nick's eyes widened as he tossed down his keys and looked her over slowly from her head to her toes. "You look gorgeous," he said in a raspy voice. He shrugged out of his coat and let it drop unheeded as he loosened and yanked off his tie. His gaze still drank in the sight of her, causing a flurry of her heart.

"Ah, Nick, I've been dreaming of this moment all day."

"This is a fantasy come true," he said in a deeper gravelly tone. "Come here," he added, drawing her to him. Her fingers flew over his buttons and in minutes his shirt lay on the floor while they kissed.

With a skipping heart, she clung to him, love for him driving her to kiss him with all the feeling she had.

She removed his belt and trousers, shoving away his briefs while he kicked off his shoes and peeled off socks. He walked her backward to the living area where he pulled her down on an area rug.

Wanting him, feeling as if he were slipping away from her and would soon be gone out of her life, she rolled him over, showering kisses from his mouth to his feet. Shifting astride him, she finally straightened as he raised her, holding her waist to pull her down on his thick rod.

She moaned with pleasure while he caressed her pouty nipples. Driven by sensation and a desperate need for him, she wanted to capture his heart, hold him in her life.

Then fears and anticipation were consumed by passion as she threw her head back, pumping, moving fast.

"Grace! Grace!" he cried her name in a husky voice.

"Ah, Nick, this is the best possible," she answered.

"Best," he repeated, and arched higher, thrusting into her and filling her.

She collapsed on him while he shuddered and pumped with his climax. Her breathing finally slowed, as did his. Holding her tightly, he rolled on his side and their legs entwined.

"What a homecoming," he whispered, stroking damp strands of hair from her face.

"I've been waiting all day for this," she admitted. "I want to make you happy."

"I'm delirious. You'll make me want to take off work by the middle of the afternoon every day."

"I hope I can keep you from going in at all tomorrow."

Fires flashed in his dark eyes and he kissed her again. She paused to run her fingers along his jaw. "Want to move to the bath?"

"Good idea," he said, standing and picking her up.

In minutes they were in the round marble tub and she was in his arms, astride him again while they kissed. She still was bound with the same urgency she had when he arrived home and he seemed to be the same. He was aroused, soon shifting her to enter her again, loving her with the ardor and energy he had had before.

It was almost two hours later when they were in each other's arms in bed after making long and leisurely love. Euphoria filled her and she pushed away all thoughts of pregnancy, deciding to wait until morning to tell him and have one more night of paradise.

"Dinner is in the oven and may be cooked to nothing. Want some smothered pheasant?"

"It's been in the oven all this time? Let's go look at this bird," Nick said, sliding out of bed and crossing the room to get his robe. Her gaze ran over his smooth, muscled back, his strong thighs, long legs and tight buns, and desire stirred again. The fear that she would soon lose him made her desperate to love and hold him.

She slid out of bed to go to her closet and get her robe. As she reached for it, Nick's arm circled her waist and he drew her warm, naked body against his own.

"Oh, Nick. That pheasant will burn to cinders," Grace said as she looked at Nick's mouth and stood on tiptoe to kiss him.

It was midnight before they got to the kitchen to eat. She looked at a shriveled pheasant and they made thick sandwiches out of cold chicken and pale cheese. They sat across from each other in the kitchen while they ate and she had part of her sandwich and her glass of cold milk before her appetite vanished completely.

"Come here," Nick said, turning on music and pulling her into his arms to dance around the kitchen. He danced her into the dining room. The lights were out and they could view the lights of the sprawling metropolis beyond the surrounding glass walls.

She smiled at Nick as he watched her. "This is a super marriage, Grace. Great, far beyond my anticipation and, I'll admit, my expectations were high."

"I agree with all my heart. I've been surprised because I

didn't expect it to be quite like this." She gave him an honest answer. While his comments gave her the perfect opening to tell him about her pregnancy, the words wouldn't come.

Thinking about the past hours and their loving, she watched his handsome features and couldn't bring an end to the night.

"The sex is just plain awesome," Nick said, brushing her temple with a kiss. "Memories of loving you disrupt my work all through the day."

"I'm glad to hear that," she said, and he kissed her lightly, then nuzzled her neck. He pulled her closer, wrapping his arms around her and holding her tightly against him as they danced.

He became aroused and carried her back to bed to make love again. It was dawn before she stifled a yawn. "Nick, we've loved all night long. It'll be time for you to go to the office soon."

He chuckled. "I may play hooky this morning and sleep in. Or have a *sex-in*."

She smiled and brushed a kiss on his shoulder. "Good plan," she said, wanting him at home. She trailed kisses across his flat belly while she caressed him, seeing he was aroused and ready.

"Insatiable and sexy," he murmured, raking his fingers in her hair. "Perfect," he added, and she caressed his throbbing manhood.

Later, she fell asleep in Nick's arms and when she stirred, she studied him. His black lashes were long with a slight curl. His lips were sensual, his lower lip full. Longing to wind her fingers in his hair, she resisted because she didn't want to wake him. She had postponed telling him her news as long as she could. Dread was a cold knot in her stomach. She couldn't shake the feeling that her condition was going to be an unwanted shock to Nick. No way could she imagine that Nick would be happy to discover he was going to become a father of another baby. He was warming to Michael more with each passing day, but he still viewed Michael as Bart's son, slightly removed from himself.

Midmorning as they finished breakfast, Nick sat across from her. He was satiated, in euphoria, yet she could arouse him with just a look or touch. It was still a honeymoon. He couldn't get enough of her and he was tempted to toss aside his responsibilities for today—something he had never done before—and take her back to bed instead of leaving for the office.

The marriage had turned out to be so much more than he had expected. He couldn't stop thinking about Grace whenever he was away from her. Sex was hot, fantastic.

He looked at her thick mane of brown hair tumbling over her shoulders, thinking how it felt to run his fingers through the silky strands.

His gaze slipped lower and he undressed her with his eyes, becoming aroused, wanting her as if they hadn't made love all night and all morning. She was beautiful, captivating, sensual. And lusty. He couldn't stop thinking about entering his condo and having her appear in nothing but heels and black lace.

She was the sexiest woman he'd ever known, the most exciting to make love to. "Come here, Grace."

Her green eyes darkened and she licked her lips, her pink tongue moving slowly across her rosy, full mouth. She stood and moved away from her chair while she continued to gaze into his eyes with a sultry look that heated him more.

She walked around the table and he gripped her wrist, tugging lightly to pull her down on his lap.

"Come sit in my lap," he said. "I told them I would be in

the office this afternoon because there are some things I need to take care of."

"You told them you'd be there before noon," she reminded him. "It's the middle of the morning now."

"Trying to get rid of me?" he teased, caressing her nape while inhaling the exotic perfume she wore.

"Not at all. Actually, I want to talk to you. You're already late going in. It won't matter if you're just a little bit later."

"I hope you have something in mind besides talk," he said.

"I do, but first, I want to talk to you," she said as he leaned closer to brush kisses on her throat.

"Talk? I had other plans," he said, pushing open the vee neck of her scarlet velvet robe.

She tilted his chin to look directly into his eyes. "I want your attention, Nick. I'll have it fully in a moment here. I have something I want to tell you."

Puzzled, he looked into worried green eyes and realized she was not only serious, but concerned about something.

"So what is this bad news?" he asked quietly, a premonition of disaster nagging at him for the first time.

"I didn't say it was bad. It's not to me."

"Then it won't be to me," he said, inhaling her scent. "So let's cut to the chase."

Placing her hands on either side of his face, she looked directly into his eyes. Her palms were cold and felt damp. "Hey," he said, reaching up to take her hands and study her intently. "You're cold. What is it, Grace?"

"Nick, I'm pregnant," she said.

Ten

Shocked, Nick inhaled as if all the breath had been knocked out of him. "You can't be. You told me you're on the Pill."

"Yes, I am. This must have happened before I got on it," she said.

"Before that, we just made love one night and I used protection," he stated, releasing her hands without thinking about what he was doing as his mind went back over their times together.

"The doctor explained to me condoms aren't foolproof, which I already knew. The statistics of failure are low, but it happens, Nick."

"You've been to the doctor already." He recalled their first night together. It seemed eons ago now. "It was Christmas Eve. You're going into the second month," he said, feeling as if a trap were closing over him. A pregnancy. His baby in their lives. He would be tied in this union that had become real, the vows binding with this pregnancy.

"That's right."

"This isn't exactly in my plans," he said, thinking aloud, almost forgetting Grace as he thought about his new status. He would be a father. His own baby. For a few moments, he forgot about being tied into this contract marriage of convenience. Instead, he considered becoming a father—the baby was his. Grace was carrying his baby. Momentarily, amazement was predominant. Then he thought of all the responsibility the baby would bring. Most of all—the permanency now of the union of the mother and father of the baby.

"It wasn't in my expectations either, but it's happened. We'll have a baby around mid-September." She slipped off his lap and walked away, pulling the neck of the robe closed beneath her chin.

She plunged her hands into the pockets and walked to the window to look outside. "We have a deal, but you've got what you wanted. In a few months we can separate. From what you've told me about your father, he'll accept it. He won't know whether we see each other or not."

"I didn't say I wanted to end our marriage, Grace. It's a shock and I'm adjusting, but you're jumping out on a limb," he said, surprised by her reaction. He crossed the room to turn her to face him. "This pregnancy isn't what either of us expected and I need to give it thought. I'm going to be a father when I thought I was getting into a marriage of convenience that would eventually end."

"Nick, we'll part ways. You're not in love and you didn't expect to become a father any more than I expected to have a baby besides Michael. It doesn't change our long-term plans. We each got what we wanted out of this marriage. You're not tied into it any more than you were yesterday before you knew about the baby."

"I think I'm definitely tied into it," he argued. "If you wanted me to jump for joy, I can't because this is a shock and not in the plans. Let me get accustomed to the idea and think about the future. We don't need to talk about ending a marriage that is good."

"Very well," she said.

He focused on her and realized she sounded subdued and she looked unhappy. He pulled her into his arms to hold her close. "Stop worrying and give me a chance to consider this. You've been thinking about it and adjusting. Give me time to do the same."

Nodding, she stood stiffly in silence and he guessed he had disappointed her. She would get over it and her natural exuberance would return. He needed some time to think about their future and this explosive news.

He was going to become a father. Amazed, he realized there was no use in looking back or wishing they had done something differently. The baby was on its way and that was that.

He thought about Michael, who would now have a sibling. That was a plus. Then he thought about his dad. Another plus because his dad would be overjoyed. "Grace, we should call Dad and go see him to tell him the news. He will be excited and joyous over another grandchild."

"Of course," she said, looking up at him and stepping out of his embrace. "I'll get dressed. You go to the office. You can call your dad and make arrangements for us to see him. He will be delighted over the news and I don't think it will upset him greatly when we part."

Nick faced her. "Grace, stop talking about ending our marriage. I haven't said one word about doing that."

"Are you ready for another baby in your life?"

"Ready or not, I'll have one early next fall."

"I doubt if you are. I think you want it all. You want a physical relationship. You want the marriage because it gives you your inheritance. You want the money, not because you need it, but because it satisfies you to win the battle. Yet you don't invest anything of yourself. You make no commitments in the relationship. The wealth itself is meaningless. You're not ready for a baby of your own. You can adopt Michael and play with him, but it's superficial. You're not really investing yourself in a deep, meaningful way," she said. "I may want out of this before you do," she added, and left.

Surprised by her accusations, he let her go. Her anger had come out of the blue and he wondered if it was caused by the discovery that she was pregnant. Or if she was furious that he hadn't been ecstatic to discover he would become a father.

Was she giving vent to tears? He was tempted to go after her. Had she expected him to act thrilled? Theirs was a marriage agreed to for business reasons, convenience, never out of love. Surely she hadn't expected him to turn cartwheels and be overjoyed at becoming a father of another baby. His baby, but a surprise.

Instead of going after Grace, he turned to the window, but he saw nothing outside. He was thinking over his future and what he needed to do to provide for this baby. *His* baby. It amazed him each time he thought about it, something he had never expected to happen. He pulled out his cell phone to call his dad.

Grace sat in a rocker in her bedroom. Tears stung. It was foolish to cry, because she shouldn't have expected a big, enthusiastic response from Nick. He hadn't been in love when they married—wasn't in love now. Words of love had never crossed his lips. He was happy in their marriage, but always in the back of his mind had to be the fact that it wasn't a permanent relationship.

She faced what really hurt. She wanted his love. She wanted Nick to love her and be overjoyed about the baby. His baby. She covered her eyes and cried quietly.

She dried her eyes and raised her chin. She would have two beautiful babies. Nick said he wasn't ending the marriage, but she wondered. She had poured her love into this relationship and it wasn't returned. She could stay and try to win his love, but did she want to? If she did, she would become more deeply in love with him.

She had to make a decision what to do. Right now she wanted to shower and dress because she expected to see Nick again before he left for the office.

Soon she was wore a tan sweater and matching slacks and had her hair tied behind her head with a silk scarf.

A slight rapping at the door made her wipe her eyes again. "Coming," she called, trying to pull herself together and hide her feelings. She didn't want Nick's pity.

She opened the door to find him standing there. Her heartbeat reminded her how she always reacted to the sight of him. He was the most handsome man she had known. Why had she been so foolish to dream he would fall in love with her and want this marriage to become real? She thought of pictures she had seen of him before she had met him and the beautiful, sophisticated, wealthy women he had socialized with before his marriage.

Why had she expected so much? She had been carried away by Nick's charm, the showering of presents on her, lust, but nothing that was deeply meaningful.

"You look beautiful," he said.

"Thank you."

"I called my dad and told him we would stop by to see him tonight."

"Fine."

"You're not happy," he said, reaching out to caress her throat. His touch was light and in spite of her hurt, the contact sizzled.

"I'm all right, Nick. This is a change in both our lives and I'm adjusting and reassessing."

"We should talk about this."

"We can later. You go to work as you planned."

He stood studying her and leaned forward to brush a kiss on her lips before he turned and left.

Watching him walk away, she closed her bedroom door. How long would it take to get over Nick?

She felt as if it would take forever. She looked around the beautiful bedroom they shared. Did she want to walk out on this or stay and take her chances? Again, she thought about the women that used to be in his life. She knew some still called him because she had heard him talking to them and politely getting rid of them. She didn't want to be one of those he politely got out of his life. Why had she ever thought she could win his heart?

Aunt Clara had warned her not to foolishly think she could gain Nick's love. Nick would not stay in a relationship because of an unplanned pregnancy; nor would he because of Michael.

Tears threatened again and she blinked them back, clamping her jaw and going to get her phone to call Aunt Clara. If they were going to see Eli tonight, she would have to pick up Michael. She also had to tell Clara about the baby.

Michael was asleep when Grace arrived at Clara's house so they went to the kitchen to talk and have a cup of hot tea.

"I've wanted to see you and have a chance to talk. I went to the doctor this week. I'm going to have a baby."

Clara shrieked and laughed, throwing her arms around Grace and causing another pang, because this was the kind of jubilant reaction she had wanted from Nick. She hugged Clara as hot tears spilled on her cheeks and her aunt pulled away. The minute she saw Grace's tears, her smile vanished.

"You're crying. Aren't you happy?"

"I'm delighted. It's Nick. He's stunned because we hadn't planned on this. Aunt Clara, common sense tells me I shouldn't expect Nick to react like a man in love would, but I want him to," she confessed.

"Oh, Grace, I was afraid of this," Clara said, hugging Grace again. While Clara returned to her seat, Grace wiped her eyes.

"I'm okay. I'm thinking about what to do. I don't know that I can stay with Nick. It's going to be difficult to stay in a relationship that is so one-sided."

"What's one-sided about it?" Clara asked, her eyes narrowing. "You're in love with Nick."

Grace nodded and wiped her eyes again, struggling to get her emotions under control.

"Darling, men like Nick—with so much wealth and accustomed to getting what he wants—some of those men probably can't settle. Nick has grown up with a terrible example in his father. Plus Nick has entered this relationship without love and so did you."

"I know. I shouldn't have expected anything else."

"Does Nick want to end this marriage?"

"No, but I don't know if I want to stay in it when his heart isn't in it."

"If you want to move in with me for a time so you can think clearly, you know I'd love having you," Clara offered.

"Thank you."

Michael's cries interrupted them and Grace stood. "I'll get him. I've missed him." She picked up Michael, who reached out to her. His crying changed to a smile as he hugged her and snuggled close in her arms. "You're going to be a big brother, darling," she told him, patting his back. That was one of the great things about her pregnancy. She would have a baby,

Nick's baby, and Michael would become a big brother and have a sibling close in age.

"He had a good nap," Clara said.

"I need to take him home because I'll have to get him changed to go see Eli tonight and share the news."

"He will be overjoyed whether Nick is or not."

"I know he will."

"You will probably get showered with another priceless gift for giving him another grandchild."

"I imagine you're also correct on that assumption."

"If Nick were an ordinary man, I would say, be patient, give him time. But I don't think his attitude will change if you two stay together for the next five years."

"That's what worries me, too. If I stay, I will be so in love it will tear me to pieces to leave him or for him to leave me. Right now, it will hurt, but hopefully, I'll get over it."

"I can promise you, you'll get over it," Clara said. "You haven't known Nick long enough to be truly, deeply in love with the kind of love that is devastating when it ends."

The words stung and Grace remained silent, but she doubted that her aunt was correct. The way she felt now, she expected to love Nick the rest of her life.

She told Clara goodbye and drove home to get Michael ready for his visit to his grandfather.

As she was finishing Michael's bath, Nick appeared in the doorway. "Let me take over," he said, tossing his coat and tie on a chair. He returned, rolling up his sleeves to wave her away.

Watching Nick finish Michael's bath, her insides knotted again. Nick was marvelous with Michael and before long Michael was going to love him and look to him as his father.

Nick grabbed a towel, tossing it over his shoulder. He picked up Michael to stand him on the edge of the tub and wrap the towel around him, talking and playing with him all the time he dried him. They looked like father and son to her. The black-haired man and the black-haired, brown-eyed child.

Shortly, Nick had Michael dressed and ready and they left to see Eli. As she watched Eli talk to Michael and hold him, she knew whatever happened, she would never take the babies away from Eli. While he hadn't helped Alicia, he hadn't been the one who turned Alicia away.

"Dad, we came by to tell you some news we have."

"And what is that?" Eli asked, looking from Nick to her.

"Grace is expecting your second grandchild."

Michael climbed down off Eli's lap and crawled to get a toy while Eli's eyes sparkled and he stood. "Congratulations! That's the best news you could possibly bring me. I'm delighted," he said, shaking Nick's hand and crossing the room to Grace. She stood to hug him lightly and he embraced her in return. He smiled at her. "You've made me happier than you'll ever know."

Megan entered the room and Eli motioned to her. "Megan, come hear the news. I'm going to have a new grandchild. I will be the grandfather of two."

"How wonderful!" Megan exclaimed, hugging Grace lightly and smiling at Nick. "Congratulations! That is really great."

"Let's drink a toast, if you don't mind lemonade or tea, Grace."

"Not at all," she said, thinking everyone's reaction had been joyous with the exception of the one person in the world she wanted to be thrilled over the news.

Eli raised his glass in a toast. "Here's to my grandchildren." He touched her glass with his and then took a long drink before setting down his glass. She sipped hers. "Another grandchild. I am ecstatic. A grandchild is special beyond measure. A grandchild is unconditional love. Probably the only relationship on earth like that. Even on a honeymoon, there's really no such thing as unconditional love. If I were younger, I would be dancing you around the room," he said, and she laughed. He held up his hand. "Just a moment. This is a special occasion and calls for something special in return. I'll be right back," he said on his way out of the room.

They chatted with Megan until Eli returned, crossing the room to Grace. "Grace, you've made my life happy and I love my grandson. Now I have the joy of looking forward to another grandchild. I want you to have this to remember this night and my gratitude. It was my grandmother's. It will go with your green eyes."

Eli handed her a box that had a worn corner. She opened it and gasped. "Eli, this is beautiful," she said, picking up a bracelet made of diamonds and emeralds.

"I want you to have it and I hope you like it. Thank you for Michael and for the next baby."

Both Megan and Nick went to look at the bracelet and then Nick fastened it on her wrist.

"It's beautiful," she said, looking at the glittering gems.

Eli returned to his chair. The rest of the evening, Grace noticed, he had a smile on his face.

Later, on the way home in the car, she looked at the bracelet on her wrist. "Nick, this bracelet is gorgeous and should stay in your family."

"Grace, you are in my family now. You're my wife, mother of my child and mother of Bart's baby. You are part of the Rafford clan."

"I felt funny accepting this in front of Megan."

"No need to. Megan gets a princely sum for her salary. Besides, haven't you noticed—Megan is only fifteen years younger than my dad. They enjoy each other's company.

I suspect Megan has already received some fancy baubles herself."

"I hadn't noticed. Well, I suppose I have noticed they get along and your dad enjoys her company."

"I think Megan enjoys his, too."

They turned into the garage of the condo and she forgot about Eli and Megan.

Michael had already fallen asleep and shortly he was tucked in his crib. When she returned to their bedroom, Nick drew her into his arms to kiss her and for the night, their problems diminished.

They made love through the night and Grace was passionate, feeling as if they might not have many more nights together.

The following week Grace packed her things and Michael's. Nick had been out of town and was due back in Dallas midafternoon. She expected him to go by the office and get home at five. She'd taken Michael to Clara's and now waited for Nick.

She had dressed conservatively, wearing a navy jacket and slacks with a short-sleeved navy sweater, her hair tied behind her head. As she put a suitcase in her car, Nick pulled into his parking spot and climbed out.

"Don't you do that," he said, crossing the few yards to pick up her other suitcase and put it in the back of her car, which already held three suitcases.

"You're going somewhere?"

Her throat knotted. "Yes, I am."

He glanced around. "Let's go inside," he said, and she nodded, walking in silence beside him.

"Did you have a successful trip?"

"Yes. I acquired the land I wanted. Details will have to

be worked out by my staff, but I had a good trip. Where's Michael?"

"He's with Aunt Clara."

They entered the condo and Nick glanced around. "Any staff here?"

She shook her head. "We're alone."

"You look great," he said. "Why the suitcases?"

"Nick, I think I should move out for a while. At least, I want to separate for a time to think things over and decide about the future."

He frowned. "Why? And not while you're pregnant. You should stay until after the baby is born."

"I don't think so. I might come back, but I want out for now," she said, afraid the control she had over her emotions would give way and she would cry. "My move won't jeopardize your seeing Michael if you want to, or Eli seeing Michael."

"'You know I'm good for Michael."

"You can see Michael whenever you want."

"I don't understand why you're doing this. Is this because I was shocked over the news we're having a baby?" Nick asked.

"Not your shock. I was shocked, too. I don't think you want to be a dad to two. Actually, I can't do this relationship without a commitment from you."

"We're married, Grace. That's legally binding."

"We're wed, but it isn't a real obligation. You've told me that over and over." She gave him a direct look. "I want it all. I've fallen in love with you," she admitted, barely able to get her voice. "I want your love in return. Otherwise, I don't want to stay."

Silence fell while they looked at each other and for just a moment her heart drummed with hope and anticipation that he would again ask her to stay or make some kind of declaration.

Instead, he stared at her in silence until he finally tilted his head to one side.

"Grace, I can't give you the declaration you want. Or the full marriage. I'm just not ready for that. This baby wasn't planned. I can't automatically fall in love. I'm leery of a real commitment after watching all the shallow relationships my dad has had."

They gazed at each other in silence and she could feel the clash of wills and see the wrath in Nick's dark eyes.

"Damn it," he whispered, and pulled her close to kiss her.

Angry and hurt, trying to resist him, Grace stood stiffly while he kissed her. Then his tongue stroking hers rekindled fires. She wrapped her arm around his neck and kissed him in return and was hopelessly carried away by passion. Finally, she ended the kiss and stepped away from him. "You know my cell number. I can afford what I want. I have a condo not far from Aunt Clara. She asked me to stay with her, but I wanted my own place. I need time and space to think about the future," she said.

She left and he didn't stop her. By the time she reached her car, she was blinded by tears and hoped she wasn't making a huge mistake. Crying, she drove to her condo in a gated area filled with tall oaks. Once inside her place, she sat crying, hating the loneliness and the silence, but she had to get a grip on her emotions if she wanted to go visit her aunt. She thought about Nick, standing in his back entrance, his charcoal jacket unbuttoned and his tie loosened. He had looked angry, hurt, yet incomparably appealing. She was going to miss him dreadfully and if she wanted to go back, she should return soon because it wouldn't take Nick long to move on with his life.

Each time she considered stepping back into a loveless marriage, hot sex or not, she didn't want to do it. She wanted

Nick's love and his heart was locked away behind impossible barriers that she hadn't managed to overcome.

"I love you, Nick," she whispered, crying softly and already missing him terribly.

Nick stood in the empty entry hall, staring after Grace. He was hurt and he was angry over her leaving. She was being unreasonable, ridiculous. If she wanted his love, why didn't she stay and give their marriage a chance?

He knew the answer to his own question. Because she wanted his love. He'd told her from the first that he wasn't into a lasting commitment. "Damn it," he swore. He hated her leaving, particularly at this time. She was pregnant and she ought to stay until after the baby was born and let him help with Michael and then with both babies. Michael was only eight months old now. The babies would be close in age and she would need help.

He reassured himself that Grace had enough money to hire a nanny and a cook and whoever else she wanted. He left, heading back to the club and not wanting to stay home alone.

Two weeks later he lay in the darkness staring into space. He hadn't slept peacefully since the night Grace walked out. He didn't know how many times he had picked up his phone to call her, thought about it and put away the phone. It was pointless. Neither of them would change.

He turned to look at the empty bed beside him, seeing Grace, remembering her smiling at him, kissing him, recalling the touch and feel of her body. He groaned and sat up. He'd tried working out for hours and pouring himself into business, but he couldn't keep his mind on his work. Anything to forget her, but he couldn't. His dad asked about her constantly and mentioned her and Michael's visits.

Nick had seen her when she had dropped Michael off three or four times and they had spoken coolly. She was coming tomorrow to bring Michael. Each time he saw her, Nick's heart had lurched violently. She looked gorgeous and still had her figure. There was no way yet by looking to tell she was pregnant.

Groaning again, he raked his fingers through his hair. He missed her. He admitted it to himself. He missed Michael. Seeing Michael once a week was different from living in the house with him and seeing him daily except when he traveled. He missed both of them badly.

He thought about the dinner he'd had with Tony recently. Tony had squinted his eyes and studied Nick.

"You look like hell, Nick. Why don't you try to get Grace back?"

"She doesn't want to come back. She wants it all, a real marriage. I'm not into love and real commitment."

"You look like a man in love to me."

"How would you know?" Nick snapped.

"Hey, don't take my head off. You're in love with your wife. Go get her and tell her."

Nick had glared at Tony and changed the subject, but now he mulled over the conversation. *"…you look like a man in love…you're in love with your wife…go…tell her…"* Was Tony right? Nick stared into space. Had he fallen in love with Grace? Real love? He didn't think that would ever happen to him in his entire life. It was a pitfall that he expected to avoid because it led to huge heartaches, but that's what he was suffering now. Was he actually in love with his wife? He'd never expected to fall in love, but had that made him too blind to see it?

He blinked and stared into the dark bedroom, pondering his question. It would be so simple to get her back. Tell her he loved her. Which was worse? A real commitment or this empty hell of missing her?

He had feared commitment since he was a kid and had continual upheaval in his life because of his father's failures, but he didn't have to repeat his father's mistakes. Had he cut himself off from the best relationship he could find in his lifetime?

Nick looked at his watch. It was four in the morning. He scrambled around looking for her address. He didn't want to wait—Michael never hesitated to wake her. And he wasn't declaring his love on the phone.

He paused. He was taking a giant step. This would make his marriage real and "convenience" would go out the window. He wanted Grace back in his life, so if that was love, he had to admit he had fallen in love with his wife.

The notion was startling, yet it made him feel better to think about loving her and getting her back.

He shaved and dressed, pulling on jeans and a navy sweater. The streets were empty as he followed the directions on the GPS.

At the gate, he fished out the code she had given him when he'd had to pick up Michael once. He drove in, pulled out his cell phone and called his wife.

Eleven

Grace woke to the ring of her cell phone. Instantly, thinking of Michael and Aunt Clara, she sat up in bed and grabbed her phone, becoming fully awake. The minute she answered, a deep male voice startled her.

"Grace, it's Nick."

"Nick?" she asked, puzzled, picking up her watch to look at the time. "Are you all right?" Why on earth would Nick call during the night? Had he had a car wreck? Did he need help?

"No, I'm not all right. I'm here at your door. I need to see you."

"Nick, are you sober?" she asked. She had never known him to drink to excess, but what would cause him to want to talk to her at this hour?

"Cold sober. Come to the door and let me in before a neighbor calls the police."

"I'm coming," she said, scrambling out of bed and grabbing

her red velvet Christmas robe. She glanced in the mirror at herself. Her hair was tangled and in disarray and she looked sleepy. As she hurried to the front door, she tried to comb her hair slightly with her fingers, gave it up and finally unlocked and opened the front door.

Nick stepped in. He wore a leather jacket and he looked handsome enough to make her weak in the knees.

"What is it, Nick?" she asked. "What's happened?"

He stepped in, closed the door, then reached for her, pulling her to him to kiss her hard and passionately.

Her heart slammed against her ribs and she couldn't catch her breath. She had one startled moment and then she was on fire. Desire blazed, a hungry need that tore through her like a raging wildfire. She embraced him, arching her hips against him, kissing him back while her pulse pounded.

In minutes they had peeled away each other's clothes, trying to get rid of all barriers and finally made love in her entryway with urgency tearing at them as Nick picked her up and she locked her long legs around him.

Later, he let her slide to stand. "Where's a bed?" he asked.

Picking up her robe to hold it in front of her, she squinted her eyes. "Nick, why are you here?"

He looked down at her and a muscle worked in his jaw. "I want you back. I want you to come home. I love you, Grace."

Her heart thudded and she wondered if she had heard correctly. "Nick, if you are just saying the words to get me back—"

"I love you. I mean it. I want you in my life. I'm making a commitment right now. Come home."

She felt as if a crushing burden had been lifted off her heart. "Nick, I love you," she cried, wrapping her arms around his neck and kissing him hard.

Epilogue

Grace stood on the verandah, greeting guests while children played on swings on the grassy lawn. She held a sleeping baby in her arms and smiled at Nick as he walked up to her.

"How's the little princess?" Nick asked, looking at the baby.

"She's sleeping and might sleep right through the first party she's ever attended."

"She will have plenty more," Nick said.

"Where is the prettiest baby in Texas that we've been hearing about?" Tony and Jake walked up to join them. Both men smiled at Grace as they said hello. "Let's see this little doll."

"You guys know nothing about babies, but even so, you'll have to admit this one is adorable," Nick said, turning his daughter so his friends could see her face.

One-month-old Emily Rafford yawned, opened big green eyes and gazed up at her daddy. Her wavy black hair had a tiny pink hair bow fastened in it and her pale blue dress with white embroidery made her look like a beautiful doll.

All three men studied the tiny baby. "I don't know anything about babies," Jake said, "but this is a pretty one. I'll agree."

"The two of you may know the oil business and real estate and high finance, but babies—you are both know-nothings," Nick joked, and his friends grinned.

"Never thought I'd live to see the day Nick Rafford became domesticated," Jake said, and they all laughed with Grace. She liked his friends and suspected they were as against commitment as Nick had been. She had no intention of matchmaking or meddling in the life of either one. They were charming and handsome, but not nearly as charming and handsome to her as the man she married.

Nick placed his arm lightly across her shoulders and moved close.

"Now where is Michael?" Tony asked. "We'll say hello to him."

Nick pointed. "At the swings with Grace's aunt Clara."

"We'll go see if we can relieve Aunt Clara," Tony said. Both men strolled away, their long legs covering the sloping lawn.

She looked around at the mansion that Nick had built for her, letting her decorate. Nick had also built a house on the grounds for Clara.

When Grace turned to smile at Nick, his arm tightened around her shoulders. "Here comes Megan and I know she is going to want to take Emily to Dad, so I'll go deliver her now."

Grace watched Megan take Emily from Nick and head in Eli's direction while Nick strolled back. "Quick, before someone else comes up, you come with me. I need you to look at something."

"Nick, you aren't just trying to escape talking to guests for a few minutes, are you?" she asked, amused and suspecting that was exactly the case.

Holding his hand, she went with him to the library. He pulled her inside and closed the door, turning to lean against it and take her in his arms.

"At last," he announced. "I want you and I don't want to wait."

She smiled at him. "I quite agree. Let them hunt for their host and hostess for just a few minutes while I kiss my dashing husband."

"Dashing? I don't know about that. Now beautiful, gorgeous, sexy wife—that's on target. I adore you and I want you. Come here." He kissed her and she tightened her arms around his neck.

Joy filled her as she held the man she loved with all her heart. While her heart drummed with devotion, she was secure and happy in the knowledge that she not only had two beautiful children, but also that Nick loved her and meant what he said.

* * * * *

COMING NEXT MONTH

Available December 7, 2010

#2053 THE TYCOON'S PATERNITY AGENDA
Michelle Celmer
Man of the Month

#2054 WILL OF STEEL
Diana Palmer
The Men of Medicine Ridge

#2055 INHERITING HIS SECRET CHRISTMAS BABY
Heidi Betts
Dynasties: The Jarrods

#2056 UNDER THE MILLIONAIRE'S MISTLETOE
"The Wrong Brother"—Maureen Child
"Mistletoe Magic"—Sandra Hyatt

#2057 DANTE'S MARRIAGE PACT
Day Leclaire
The Dante Legacy

#2058 SWEET SURRENDER, BABY SURPRISE
Kate Carlisle

REQUEST YOUR FREE BOOKS!

2 FREE NOVELS PLUS 2 FREE GIFTS!

Silhouette Desire®

Passionate, Powerful, Provocative!

HARLEQUIN®

A Romance

FOR EVERY MOOD™

Spotlight on

Classic

Quintessential, modern love stories
that are romance at its finest.

See the next page
to enjoy a sneak peek from
the Harlequin® Romance series.

See below for a sneak peek from our classic
Harlequin® Romance® line.

Introducing DADDY BY CHRISTMAS by Patricia Thayer.

MIA caught sight of Jarrett when he walked into the open lobby. It was hard not to notice the man. In a charcoal business suit with a crisp white shirt and striped tie covered by a dark trench coat, he looked more Wall Street than small-town Colorado.

Mia couldn't blame him for keeping his distance. He was probably tired of taking care of her.

Besides, why would a man like Jarrett McKane be interested in her? Why would he want to take on a woman expecting a baby? Yet he'd done so many things for her. He'd been there when she'd needed him most. How could she not care about a man like that?

Heart pounding in her ears, she walked up behind him. Jarrett turned to face her. "Did you get enough sleep last night?"

"Yes, thanks to you," she said, wondering if he'd thought about their kiss. Her gaze went to his mouth, then she quickly glanced away. "And thank you for not bringing up my meltdown."

Jarrett couldn't stop looking at Mia. Blue was definitely her color, bringing out the richness of her eyes.

"What meltdown?" he said, trying hard to focus on what she was saying. "You were just exhausted from lack of sleep and worried about your baby."

He couldn't help remembering how, during the night, he'd kept going in to watch her sleep. How strange was that? "I hope you got enough rest."

She nodded. "Plenty. And you're a good neighbor for

coming to my rescue."

He tensed. Neighbor? *What neighbor kisses you like I did?* "That's me, just the full-service landlord," he said, trying to keep the sarcasm out of his voice. He started to leave, but she put her hand on his arm.

"Jarrett, what I meant was you went beyond helping me." Her eyes searched his face. "I've asked far too much of you."

"Did you hear me complain?"

She shook her head. "You should. I feel like I've taken advantage."

"Like I said, I haven't minded."

"And I'm grateful for everything…"

Grasping her hand on his arm, Jarrett leaned forward. The memory of last night's kiss had him aching for another. "I didn't do it for your gratitude, Mia."

Gorgeous tycoon Jarrett McKane has never believed in Christmas—but he can't help being drawn to soon-to-be-mom Mia Saunders! Christmases past were spent alone…and now Jarrett may just have a fairy-tale ending for all his Christmases future!

Available December 2010, only from Harlequin® Romance®.

Silhouette Desire

USA TODAY bestselling authors

MAUREEN CHILD

and

SANDRA HYATT

UNDER THE MILLIONAIRE'S MISTLETOE

Just when these leading men thought they had it all figured out, they quickly learn their hearts have made other plans. Two passionate stories about love, longing and the infinite possibilities of kissing under the mistletoe.

Available December wherever you buy books.

Always Powerful, Passionate and Provocative.

Visit Silhouette Books at www.eHarlequin.com

SD73069

HARLEQUIN Presents